SPEAMAN'S GRASS

John Wells had given up sheriffing to be a troubleshooter for his commanding officer of yesteryear, General Amos Spearman. He hadn't been on Spearman's grass for an hour when he saw the evidence of a most bitter conflict. But did the farmers have the right to the grass that the cowmen had fought and bled for? Wells found his answer when an old man shot a young and unfaithful wife, and he was able to pluck a child out of the air just one yard short of oblivion.

DAN ROYAL

SPEARMAN'S GRASS

Complete and Unabridged

LINFORD
Leicester

First published in Great Britain in 1988 by
Robert Hale Limited
London

First Linford Edition
published 1999
by arrangement with
Robert Hale Limited
London

British Library CIP Data

Royal, Dan, *1928* –
    Spearman's grass.—Large print ed.—
Linford western library
    1. Western stories
    2. Large type books
    I. Title
    823.9′14 [F]

    ISBN 0–7089–5555–X

Published by
F. A. Thorpe (Publishing) Ltd.
Anstey, Leicestershire

Set by Words & Graphics Ltd.
Anstey, Leicestershire
Printed and bound in Great Britain by
T. J. International Ltd., Padstow, Cornwall

This book is printed on acid-free paper

1

John Wells had not felt this free in a long time. There was rock about to be sure, but the prairie was wide and the early summer sky was a great arch of cloudless blue. As he had ridden north, the last of that feeling of responsibility and restriction had worked out of his system and he had the knowledge that, for now anyway, the twenty four hours of the day were his own.

The law was a hard master. It treated even the least embattled of its servants like slaves; and it had treated John Wells, lately the sheriff of Crowbank, Texas, like an absolute beast of burden. For among the many doorways to hell upon this earth, Crowbank was second to none. What between the eternally brawling troopers who inhabited the fort nearby and the gun-crazy cowboys from the ranches of the border country, there had been job enough, but when you added in the dissolute scum resident in the town itself and the fact that Crowbank was the natural dormitory for the lawless traffic to and from Mexico that used nearby El Paso all the year round, the work was never-ending and the sheriff's life constantly at risk. Yes, sirree! Policing Crowbank had been no sinecure, and he was thoroughly glad to be shut of the task.

Not that he believed for one moment that he was riding towards a rest cure now. The man for whom he was going to work, General Amos Spearman, was a shrewd man with a dollar, and he was not given to offering the kind of salary that he had mentioned in his letter of a month ago if he did not expect to extract his full money's-worth from the recipient.

Neither was Wells, when it came right down to it, one hundred percent happy about what he was doing; for it seemed that the general was having trouble with nesters and was hiring Wells' gun and all-round expertise to help deal with it. Normally, the ex-sheriff would not have looked at the kind of work that Spearman had put his way. He hated the Graze Laws. They created more problems than they solved. Nobody had ever exactly defined a homesteader's rights or what constituted pre-emption. It was all very fine for Washington to grant John Citizen, farmer, land to till, when John Citizen, rancher, had already been grazing the selfsame land for ten or fifteen years. The farmer might say that he had the full power of the government of the United States behind him, but that did not make his right to the disputed land any greater than that of the man who had got there first and perhaps fought the Indians for the grass. Anyway, John Wells could not see that it did.

'What do you reckon, horse?' he asked of the buckskin stud that he was forking. 'Does a hoe-man have the unquestioned right to put his plough into soil that his neighbour bled for just because those officials way back East say he has?'

The horse snorted — which, being translated, no doubt meant that it didn't give a damn. Horses had more sense than to muddle their heads with questions of right and wrong. Food, water, and space to live with the rest of Creation was all they required. Oh, sure! They fought for the right to breed, but that insured that only the best blood came through. Beyond that, they let time and Nature take their course, and got along very nicely, thank you.

'Dead right,' Wells opined. 'But you remember General Spearman. He's a rare one, and we always found him as fair and straight as a man can be. If he's satisfied that his cause is just, we may feel sure also. That means there'll be no dishonour to us in serving it.'

Sounded right good. Yet he was still conscious that he was talking to convince himself. With all his faith in

4

Spearman — and his own belief in his ability to judge what was right for himself — he could not forget that the general was only human and had always been acquisitive and conservative in the extreme. Try as he would, he could not fully rid himself of that special strain of self-doubt which had been unsettling his mind. He had told himself that friendship and his desire to help in another's troubles had been the main reason for his resignation as Crowbank's sheriff, but had he in fact been looking for a way out whatever the cost and simply made a reckless grab? If the former were the whole truth, then his judgment was acceptable and his integrity whole, but if the latter, it could mean that he had let his need for change warp the morality in which his parents had raised him. He must care about others, and not let any form of selfishness make him indifferent to their rights and needs. If pandering to his own desires should prove the measure of blind service to a dubious cause, then his judgment was far from acceptable and his integrity damaged. But what the hell! A man could drive himself crazy by narrowing his mind and setting up all these question marks. Everything would become plain, and he would see that he had done right. It was always so. And who said that he had ever had the makings of a saint?

Wells eased himself in the saddle. He should be getting close to Spearman's Broken S by now. He had called on a sutler that morning, and the man had informed him that he was twenty five miles from Amarillo and about nineteen from the Spearman spread. He had been jogging along steadily since then and, if you counted the time lost on those few miles of hard climbing which had brought him to this higher range, he ought to have covered most of the nineteen by this early part of the afternoon. He would be glad to see trail's end, and he could certainly do with a good meal and a few hours rest.

Then his nostrils gave a sudden twitch, and his mind alerted to the world outside himself. He turned his head to the right, and sniffed harder, detecting the presence of woodsmoke in the air. The fumes had a steamy, sooty odour from their mingling with water, and he received the impression that somebody not far away could have a building on fire. Lifting in his stirrups, he peered across the land, but could see nothing of building or flames, though he could make out declining ground a short distance to the north of him and suspected that the origins of the woodsmoke probably lay on the unseen land at the bottom of the slope which tilted away to the left.

He thought it unlikely that anything disastrous had occurred, but curiosity drew him nevertheless, and he turned his horse to the right and soon reached the declining ground, swinging left here and following the slope down into a sizeable low. This ended against a wall of rock and grass about a quarter of a mile to the west of him, and he could see that much of the ground towards the rear of the place had been ploughed up. At the front of the area stood a log cabin — smoking at its southern end, where flames had clearly been extinguished in the last hour — and on the right of the dwelling grew a stand of silver birch trees, with a bank rising behind it towards a continuation of the high grass which he had been riding for the last hour or so on this side of the low.

Now movement caught Wells' attention. In front of the cabin and not far from the trees, he made out a woman, young, slim, and yellow-haired, who was labouring with a spade and mattock and starting to open a hole that looked suspiciously like a grave. Beyond the foot of the excavation and looking on, stood a small child, a little girl of about four-years, who was also yellow-headed, had the thumb of one hand raised to her mouth and the fingers of the other twisted into the washed-out forget-me-not blue of her dress.

Wells made the necessary adjustment to his line of travel. He headed for the cabin's open front door, though his gaze seldom left the toiling female. Suddenly the force of his stare seemed to get through to her, for she lifted from her digging, tossed back her hair, and looked up the slope towards him. Then, obviously fearing, she dropped her shovel and sprang away from the excavation, seizing and cocking a Winchester which stood against one of the nearby trees. Then she set her feet apart and pointed the rifle towards him, eyes threatening.

'You don't need that!' he called. 'I mean you no harm!'

The woman didn't answer. She went on covering him. He could see that she was putting a dangerous amount of pressure on the rifle's trigger. But he went on advancing, as if the rifle had no existence, and rode level with her and the child before reining in and answering what he now saw to be the blonde's sombre, tear-stained gaze with a smile. 'Ma'am,' he said, nodding at the beginnings of the hole on his right, 'that's no work for a woman's hands. I see you've had a fire. Would you be fixing to bury something?'

'Somebody,' she said, letting her rifle sag. 'My husband, Bill Hastings. You're not — one of them?'

'Who might they be?' Wells queried.

'Those wicked devils from the Broken S!' Mrs Hastings replied, her vehemence such that it appeared to drain her of the life force and take the legs from under her, for she went down in what was obviously a dead faint.

Wells sprang out of his saddle. He ran to the woman and knelt beside her. He turned her face from side to side, peering at it closely. Then he became aware that the little girl had moved up and was now standing near his right elbow. Glancing round at her, he saw the innocent, inquiring sweetness of the child's face and gently ruffled her curls with his right hand. 'Hello, sprout.'

'Why did mummy fall down?' the little one asked, her voice full of puzzlement that her eyes seemed to deny — as if she understood all, yet nothing that mattered.

'Your mummy's fainted, child,' Wells replied, giving the woman's face a few light slaps — which achieved no result — and then feeling for the throat pulses, which he found thready and irregular. 'Nothing to worry about. Don't you cry now. You'll frighten that old jay-bird if you do!'

Wells stood up; then, bending slightly, he picked the woman up and began carrying her in the direction of the cabin. Entering, he stopped just beyond the threshold and looked around him. The living room was small and no more than adequately furnished. He saw a table, couch, rocking-chair, two straight-backed chairs, a sideboard that was really a chest-of-drawers, a narrow bookcase that held perhaps a score of volumes, and a large, colourful rag carpet before a shingled fireplace on which a half-cooked stew had now turned to a cold and greasy paste in its saucepan. All about what you'd expect — except for the object which lay on the left of his path: for this he recognised as the body of a man sewn into a winding sheet of sackcloth. Bill Hastings, no doubt.

Keeping clear of the body, Wells moved to the hearth and there deposited the unconscious woman on the rag carpet, kneeling again himself and starting to chafe Mrs Hastings' wrists and otherwise stimulate her circulation, and after a minute her lungs drew a deep, gasping breath and her eyes fluttered open and then fixed on his, intelligence and memory slowly returning to her gaze and building into a new expression of suffering. Then her face rolled aside and she began a silent weeping.

Ignoring her grief — since it was very much a case of better out than in — Wells picked the blonde up again and carried her to the couch, lowering her gently upon it and putting a cushion behind her head. 'Lie there,' he ordered. 'You need a rest, girl. You're shocked to hell. I can see what needs to be done here. I'll do it.'

The woman looked as if she were about to protest, but Wells put on his sternest face and raised a silencing finger, turning then to find out what had become of the little girl and seeing that she, too, had entered the cabin — probably in his immediate wake — and was now gazing in a bewildered fashion at the form sewn into the sackcloth. Going to the child, Wells picked her up and bore her to the couch, placing her at her mother's feet. 'What's your name, sprout?' he asked.

'Annie,' came the quavering response.

'Got a job for you, Annie,' Wells informed her. 'I want you to take care of your mama. Okay?'

'Yes, sir,' the child replied, running into the arms that her mother opened to her.

'That's the girl!' Wells approved, winking at Mrs Hastings. 'You two'll be all right.'

Then the blonde startled him by asking: 'Are you the law?'

'No, ma'am.'

'I thank you anyway. You're a good man, Mr —'

'Wells. Nor am I sure that I'm good. Rest, eh?'

The woman said no more. Wells walked to the shrouded corpse. Then, taking a firm hold on the still limp remains, he dragged them outside as swiftly as he could, turning left beyond the door and hauling them into the trees adjacent. After that, letting go of his burden, he walked on through the stand of timber and came out at its back, finding himself on the edge of a dried-up water channel that skirted the foot of the grassy bank that stood opposite.

Wells stepped into the middle of the channel. He drove his right heel into the soil beneath it, nodding to himself as the dirt yielded readily. He ought to be able to sink a grave at this spot without taking the rest of the day over it. Anyhow, this was a better place to bury a man than within sight of the cabin's front door. It went without saying that the grave which Mrs Hastings had started to dig had been sited close to her door in recognition that she lacked the strength to drag her husband's corpse as far as this. Later, she would have regretted the burial so near her front window, for who wished to look upon even a loved one's grave at every hour of the day?

Wells threaded a return of the trees; then, coming once more to where the shrouded figure lay, fetched it back to where he meant to bury it. After that he repeated his traverse of the birch stand and emerged close to where Mrs Hastings had begun her excavation. Here he picked up the mattock and shovel she had earlier been using to dig and carried them back to the dried-up ditch, falling to work without pause and soon sinking a deep slot into the black soil present. Sweating freely, he kicked and chopped and shovelled for a while longer, widening the grave and then levelling off cleanly at about five feet down, and when he was satisfied that he had done the best he could, he climbed out of the hole, sleeved off, and rolled the corpse into it, filling in thereafter at a much faster pace than the original digging had permitted and completing the job by beating the displaced soil into a neat mound that won even his own approval.

He allowed himself a short breather; then, still oozing sweat and dragging the tools after him, he moved back into the trees, pausing suddenly in their shade and turning again in response to a compelling afterthought. 'I didn't know you, mister,' he said to the grave. 'I don't know what you looked like or how you thought. But your woman and child must be some measure of what you were, and they're okay; so I guess you were okay too. That being so, sir, I, who haven't the least right, commend your immortal part to Great God Almighty and pray you'll rest where I've put you until the Last Trumpet sounds. Fare-you-well — brother.'

Once more he turned away, and this time he was determined never to look upon the grave again unless he had to; then, trailing the mattock and shovel for the second time, he made his way back to the cabin ground and there cleaned up the soles and insteps of his boots by using the shoulders of the shovel-blade as a scraper. After that he stood the tools against the front wall of the dwelling adjacent and sauntered into the cabin's living room, knocking on the door after he had bowed through the entrance. He saw immediately that Mrs Hastings was no longer resting, and the smell of fresh coffee drew his eyes to the hearth, where the woman had got a new fire burning and the grounds steeping in a much-used pot. 'I've finished out there, Mrs Hastings,' he said. 'He's lying behind the birch trees. You'll see where.'

'Thank you,' the woman said. 'Coffee?'

He nodded. It all seemed so matter-of-fact. There ought to have been a hint of drama about it, but there was nothing. She poured him his drink, and he drank some of the steaming liquid. The coffee tasted just like coffee.

'May I get you a meal, Mr Wells?' the blonde asked. 'It won't be much. Just cold beef and potatoes. Yes, and there's a slice of apple tart. Bill loved his — '

'I thank you, ma'am,' Wells hurried in, 'but no. I'm nearing where I've been headed these two weeks. I'm expecting to eat there. The coffee, though, is mighty welcome.'

'Please sit down.'

'Just for a minute then.'

She pulled out a straight-backed chair and he seated himself, twinkling the fingers of his left hand at little Annie,

18

who was watching him shyly now from a kneeling position beneath the table. 'Reckon I couldn't snuggle in there,' Wells commented.

'You're too big,' the child observed a trifle scornfully.

'I guess so,' Wells mourned. 'And too old.'

'I'm four.'

'That's a nice age to be,' he assured the child. 'I was four once. About a hundred years ago.'

'You aren't old!' Annie declared. 'you aren't any older than my — !'

'Annie,' her mother cautioned. 'You know what I've told you about little girls. They should be seen and not heard.'

'Yes, ma'am,' the child murmured, looking downcast.

'Oh, I like to hear little girls,' Wells whispered. 'Much prefer 'em to little boys. I don't half mind big girls either.'

'He's an old charmer,' the mother warned.

'Just like Charlie?' Annie wondered.

'Charlie?' Wells inquired of the woman.

'Her dog,' Mrs Hastings explained.

'He's dead,' Annie said.

'A sad fact of life,' Wells sighed. 'Child, if I remind you of Charlie, I can't be as bad as a figured I was.' He considered the woman's face now, trying to prompt her into telling him what had happened here — since he believed it was time that she did — but she failed to respond, if indeed she understood his purpose, and in the end he was forced to ask: 'What happened, Mrs Hastings? You mentioned the Broken S, if I recall.'

'Fiends!' the woman breathed. 'Amos Spearman says the land is all his. From the Scarbend limits to the Prairie river, and for five miles out towards Hereford too. Tens of thousands of acres. We came here only six months ago, on a government land grant allowing us to farm just fifty acres; but, from the first, Spearman told us that our papers were invalid so far as he was concerned.

We wrote to the Land Office in Austin, sending them a copy of our grant, and they confirmed our right to farm here at Scarbend, but Spearman still would not have it and warned us to get out. My husband went to the law office in Amarillo and told the sheriff all about it — showing his proofs, of course — but the sheriff didn't want to know and came neither near nor by.

'Bill, my husband, was furious, and contacted the Land Department in Washington, and it seems likely to me that there was some correspondence from that direction and Amos Spearman got his knuckles rapped — for the next thing we knew, Phil Baker, the Broken S's foreman, paid us a call and told us we were getting our last warning. We were to get out within the week — or else.

'That was a week ago. Phil Baker came back today. He had three men with him. We guessed what was on, and Bill went to meet them with his rifle. He shouted a warning, and Baker drew a pistol and shot him there and then. I ran to Bill, but he was already dead and, before I could do a thing about it, Baker and his companions had set fire to the cabin and ridden off. Thank goodness, they did a poor job on their fire-raising and we have a well at the back of the building and two buckets handy. I was able to extinguish the flames before they could get a real hold on the logs.

'After that, I dragged Bill's body indoors and shrouded it with the sackcloth from which we had hoped to make bags to hold our crops. Then I started trying to dig a grave. You know the rest. It was a little after that time when you came along.'

'Bad,' Wells mused. 'But it follows a familiar pattern. Where did you and your husband come from?'

'Illinois. The Hastings family isn't unknown on the lake.'

'I see,' Wells said. 'City folk with a yen for the land. Chicago? No countryman bred and born would have stepped out to meet four enemies with a rifle in his hands. He'd have shouted his warning from behind cover. Your husband gave the leader of that bad bunch a passable excuse to kill him.'

'Bill didn't want to harm anybody.'

'I don't suppose he did, ma'am. Trouble is, the law would be hard put to prove that Spearman's foreman didn't shoot in self-defence. Especially with you admitting that your man held a rifle, and three witnesses lying through their back-teeth for this Baker guy.'

'They've burned out other nesters,' the blonde said bitterly. 'There's been at least one other killing, and several woundings. They burn everything. Even those settlers who give up without a fight see their homes and possessions burned.'

'Part of the scheme,' Wells pointed out. 'There's no sense coming back if there's nothing to come back to.'

'It can't be right!' the woman choked.

'It isn't, Mrs Hastings,' Wells sighed. 'I guess things around here are much as they were over in England seven or eight hundred years ago. The cattle barons are no different from the aristocratic kind. They're strong enough to take what they want and then hold it. Might is their right. And right now the central power hasn't the will or authority to challenge them. This is a big country, ma'am. It's all down to distance, time, and money. The day will come when these big cattlemen have to toe the line. But that day isn't yet.'

'You're making me feel worse,' the woman complained.

'I can see that,' Wells admitted. 'What's happened to you this day is stark tragedy. But you must see how the other side goes on.'

'You're telling me I can do nothing?'

'You'll do whatever you want to do,' Wells replied deliberately. 'If you want the best advice that anybody can give you, I'll give it you. Go back to Illinois.'

'I've fifty dollars in the world,' Mrs Hastings said. 'With care, we reckoned it enough to keep us in the necessaries until we started to sell our crops.'

'Fifty dollars might get you back to Illinois,' Wells calculated. 'I could lend you another fifty.'

'Your loan would end up as a gift.'

'So?'

'There's nothing back in Chicago.'

'You need company for a time. Help. Have you got a friend in these parts?'

Mrs Hastings shook her head. 'I've met the Enderby family who've settled over at Beacon Ridge. But I could not call them friends. You more so than they. They're in imminent danger, too, from Amos Spearman.'

'You call me friend,' Wells growled, taking a slow, deep breath; for he could not lie to her about it. Lies did no good. The man who had first spoken the proverb concerning the tangled web had got it right. He must tell her the truth about himself; and now. 'Friend? Until tomorrow, ma'am.'

'What do you mean?'

'I'm due to join General Spearman's troubleshooters,' Wells explained. 'When you take a man's pay, you have to do his work.'

The woman turned her back on him. She gazed out of the window in the cabin's rear wall at the newly turned soil beyond the glass. 'I'm grateful,' she said after a moment. 'You have been kind. But please go. And don't come back.'

Wells rose to his feet, then set his coffee mug on the table. He had realized that it must turn out like this. 'I'm sorry, ma'am,' he said; and so he was. But it didn't change anything.'

2

Wells had lost that carefree feeling of an hour or two back as he rode away from the sheltered place in which the Hastings cabin stood. He truly felt for the new widow and her fatherless child — not least in terms of his guilt for what he had been forced to say at the end — but, as he put miles between him and the scorched cabin, he was finally compelled to remind himself that he must function as an alert individual and could not hold himself responsible for the world and its tragedies. Today he had ridden into somebody else's story and played the part allotted to him there. That must be the end of it. He was just an average guy who was required to get by in the best manner that he could, which must often mean following the dreams of a mind other than his own and being forced to do things that went against the grain. There was no perfect situation. This way or that, a man had to take sides. and he had taken Amos Spearman's when he had accepted the general's offer of work.

Suddenly Wells cut a ranch trail. His bump of direction told him that the track would take him where he wished to go. He followed the beaten way northwards, and it bore him between aged walls of outcropping stone and higher yet, bringing him to a last ridge from which he gazed to his right and down onto miles of undulating prairie. Big herds of cows smudged and blotted the pale green of the season's new grass, sprawling into creek and river bottoms, and he did not doubt that he was surveying the mid-kingdom of the Broken S, or that the large house and loose circle of ranch buildings in the foreground were where he would find the hand of an old friend and a comfortable billet. Things were set fair; here was his new start. What he had seen so far he must now ignore, and what he had heard he must forget. Here Amos Spearman was the master, and loyalty was the order of the day. He had come to do a job, and he would do it. Widows he had seen in plenty. Women were tougher than men; they survived. And small girls with bewildered faces grew into — No. That one really did hurt, and the hurt wouldn't go away. What ought to be easy for a man like him wasn't going to be so easy. Damn John Wells for a soft-hearted fool!

The trail left the caprock. It started down the western face of the ridge. Wells put his horse to the descent. Moving at a pace which did not put his mount's footing in jeopardy, he rode towards the bench at the middle of the downhill path, forking off to the right at this spot and then gigging up a bit more pace as he passed onto the long, northward-facing slope that met the edge of the ranch site below. He made a slight show of his approach, for he could see ranchmen watching his movements, and he knew that his fellow Texans liked to see a new man riding in as if he could tell one end of his horse from the other.

Thus, with the slope getting shallower, Wells sent his buckskin stretching for the ranch yard and, a minute or two later, came up tight where no harm could be done and then walked the stallion towards the main corral, where a neat-looking little man — nutbrown of skin, black-eyed, straight of nostril, square-chinned and moustachioed — had just dismissed a small knot of companions and was eyeing him with an air of authority which became more noticeable by the moment. Then, stepping away from the corral rails, the little man put up a staying hand, and Wells reined in within six feet of the other and sat gazing down at him.

'What's your business here?' came the inquiry.

'Who's asking?' Wells countered, politely enough.

'Evan Rank, segundo.'

'John Wells. The general gave me a job by post. I'm up from the Rio Grande.'

The little man's handsome features relaxed into a grin. 'Heard of you. The lawman, yes?'

'Yes.'

'Pass City, wasn't it?'

'Hell, no!' Wells chuckled, obeying the segundo's signal to dismount. 'Nothing so exalted.'

'Nothing so what?'

'Grand, Mr Rank. Bug-hole, called Crowbank. Not far from El Paso, yes. I got my share of tough characters.'

'I've heard,' the under-foreman admitted dryly. 'You may find some of them here. Amos Spearman only employs the best and hardest. So long as you remember that you're not a sheriff any more.'

'I've had a bellyful of that,' Wells said.

'I'll believe that when I've seen it,' Rank commented. 'Once a lawman, always a lawman. First sign you think you're still wearing a tin star and out you go. There's only one power here, under the general's, and its name's Phil Baker. He's a big man who doesn't like other big men. Particularly ones who may be even faster on the draw than he is and perhaps be able to dust him off.'

'You don't like him?'

Evan Rank shrugged. 'I don't like big guys. You can see why.'

'As to that,' Wells remarked, 'I've always held that the best things come wrapped in little parcels.'

'Well, now,' the segundo said in some surprise. 'I do believe you'll get on here.'

'Won't be my fault if I don't,' Wells promised. 'When do I get to see General Spearman?'

Rank glanced towards the house. 'Knew you before, didn't he?'

'In the Army. I was his top scout.'

'I'll take you to him,' the under-foreman said. 'You rate, mister. There's been an order to look out for you these ten days now.'

'Bless his old heart,' Wells said.

'Not so much of the old, Jack,' Rank advised. 'Amos, the widower of several years, took himself a new bride not so long ago. She's young and she's pretty, and she's raised his comb. Yes, sir!'

'Hope for us yet.'

'I do all right, Jack,' Rank said, winking slyly. 'You come to Amarillo with me. Turn that big horse into the corral, and we'll get over to the house.'

Wells did as commanded, then fell in behind Evan Rank. He let the little man lead him towards the ranch house, with its gambrel roof, balconies upstairs, bay windows down, and marble portico facing east — the whole indicating wealth if not taste — and they were nearing an open door in the northern wall, when a very tall and narrow-shouldered man came striding out to meet them, his right hand extended and a smile on his thin leathery face, which was further sharpened by his white goatee beard and ice-blue eyes. 'John, my boy!' he greeted. 'How good it is to see you again after all these years!'

Wells took the proffered hand and shook it warmly. 'Same goes for you, sir. You're looking well.'

Spearman patted the suspicion of a paunch which bulged into the front of his check shirt. 'Shows, doesn't it? Madeleine says she's going to cut my rations. Told her I'd go and live with the horses if she did.'

Wells chuckled obligingly, but diplomatically passed no word.

'I expect you've heard about Madeleine,' the general probed.

'I told him about her, sir,' Rank said.

'Evan, you're a damned gossip!' Spearman chided good-naturedly.

'I guess we envy you, sir,' Wells said.

'You'll envy me all the more when you see her, John,' Spearman crowed. 'She's a lovely young woman.' Then he underwent what appeared to be an abrupt change of mood. 'Poor Jane. You will remember my first wife. She died of cholera in Seventy-seven. A good woman. I still miss her, John. She belonged to my time. But I never was a man to live alone and mope.'

'I remember your first wife, sir,' Wells assured him. 'A brave lady, with a great sense of fun — and most kind.'

'They had virtues, that older school,' the general acknowledged, something in his manner suggesting for an instant that the younger breed of woman could be lacking in this respect. Then his eyes dropped towards the worn elm stock of the Frontier Model Colt that his new employee wore holstered about level with the joint of his right hip. 'Are you as good as ever with that forty-five, John?'

Frowning, Wells touched his gun. 'I believe so.'

'We'd better understand each other fully,' Spearman said, his mood now totally grave. 'I shall expect you to use that weapon when called upon. We have a situation on the Spearman grass that I could very well do without. It was none of my making, but it must be eliminated.'

'I saw something of it as I rode here from the Lubbock direction,' Wells admitted. 'I had to stop and bury the husband of a woman named Hastings.'

Spearman paled visibly, then began to fidget. 'Joan Hastings,' he murmured. 'I heard about Bill Hastings' death from Phil Baker, my foreman. Hastings threatened my man. What could Baker do but shoot him?'

'Then try to burn down the home of the man's missus and her little girl?'

'That sounded like criticism, John,' the general snapped. 'Baker carried out a standard practice. You know as well as I why a nester's home has to be burned down. They have

36

no right to break the land. I fought the Comanche for this grass. I've seen cruel winters, drought, herd pestilence, and markets that gave me a loss. I've suffered to build this ranch, and I don't intend to give up what I've fought and suffered for just because some Washington Jack-in-Office refuses to accept that my boundaries remain expansible and tries to draw arbitrary lines on his map of Texas.' He paused for breath, hands and beard working now. 'But, having said all that, John, you must believe that the last thing I want is to inflict death and suffering on a pack of ignorant would-be farmers. I'm sorry that men have died or been wounded during my campaign against these nesters, but they pointed their firearms first and my men were forced to shoot. The Constitution confers the right on a citizen to carry arms, and it also gives him the right to protect himself and his property with those arms. My men have done no more than that in my name.'

'Quite a speech, sir,' Wells acknowledged.

'Are you about to give me an argument, John?' Spearman asked in tones of warning.

'Sir, if I had that in mind I wouldn't be here.'

'It's all a matter of interpretation.'

'How you see it, yes.'

'I wish I didn't know you quite so well,' the general said frostily. 'You always did have an annoying tendency to take the part of the underdog. I suppose that was what made a lawman of you. But life is about growth and initiative, and it's time you came to an adult understanding of the world in which you live. It's all there for the taking, John, and effort is the justification. The strong are the rulers of the weak. That's how it always was and ever will be.'

'That's the rest of the speech, eh, General?' Wells inquired, bridling inwardly despite himself. 'Might is right. I knew it.'

'If you don't like what I say — '

'I can leave,' Wells interrupted.

'I don't want that, John,' Spearman said hastily. 'I regard you as a friend, and I invited you here in that spirit. You gave up a living for me. I owe us both the chance to make your job here last.'

'All right,' Wells said. 'There's no denying I need the work, and I've no quarrel with most of what you've said. This isn't a perfect world, and there's no way of making it one. Your battle is presently being fought all over the West, and it will get more violent as Washington tries to spread all our new immigrant population around.'

'You're with me?'

'Yes, sir.'

'All the way?'

'I'll know when I see where that is,' Wells said carefully. 'As far as you can reasonably expect anyhow.'

Spearman smiled a wry, shrewd smile. 'I'll have to be content with that. Very well. Evan Rank will find you a place in the bunkhouse, and I'll see you — such times as we meet around the ranch.' He glanced towards the corral. 'Is that big stallion your horse?'

'It is.'

'A fine brute, John. You always were a good judge of horseflesh. It's come a long way. Give it a feed of grain, with my compliments. You'll find plenty of corn in the stable bins.'

'I thank you, General,' Wells responded. 'So does my horse.'

Grunting, Spearman gave his beard a tug and turned away, nodding to himself as he walked back into his home. Wells watched his new employer disappear, then glanced at Evan Rank, who said: 'You walk a mighty tight rope, Jack. Slacken it off some. 'Cos I tell you, nobody else on this ranch — including Phil Baker — would have got away with how you just talked up to Amos Spearman. He don't like to be questioned, y'know. Not anyhow at all.'

'There's much between that man and me,' Wells explained. 'We saw the worst of the Civil War together. But he's not the man he was at that time of day. He really cared about people when he was younger.'

'That was before he married Madeleine,' Rank said significantly. 'Oh, heck! The man's right. I am a gossip. Come on, Jack. I'll show you the bunkhouse and the boss's stables.'

'Okay,' Wells said.

Rank turned to the right. He set off in a determined fashion towards the two buildings on that side — both very large — which stood closest to the house. The first, identified by its half-doors, was obviously the stables, while the second, remarkable for its length and the dog-trot that extended along its front, could only be the crew's quarters. 'You'll find what you want for your horse in there,' the segundo advised, pointing in the direction of the stables while heading for the bunkhouse. 'Don't let that bronc of yours get ideas above his station. Our horses — and that includes him — rough it between grass and water.'

'He's been spoiled some already,' Wells admitted, as they passed into the somewhat airless bunkhouse, with its facing rows of wooden beds, cupboards, and sets of scrubbed forms and tables. 'A town sheriff doesn't do a whole lot of riding. Not more than he can help anyway.'

'You're soft,' Rank observed, his voice holding a touch of malice. 'We'll toughen you up. There's plenty of hard work here. It's fine to be hired gun, but you won't lead the life of Riley much of the time. Amos Spearman insists on his troubleshooters earning their keep rangewise. Come the fall round-up, you'll sweat.'

'I'm not a cowhand,' Wells said, following the segundo now towards the farthest bed in the line at the rear of the dormitory and giving a nearby cupboard a light but echoing kick. 'You'll have to teach me.'

'I'll teach you,' Rank promised, flashing his white teeth. 'You can sleep here. This last bunk was mine one time. It's comfortable.' He jerked a thumb to his right. 'We get our chow next door. See that little room 'twixt here and the kitchen? Baker sleeps in there. Don't get on the wrong side of him, Jack. He's a ring-tailed roarer, and fearless. Good with a gun, and better with his fists. I daresay you're the man I've heard, but that don't mean you're another Baker.'

'I'll keep it in mind,' Wells assured him. 'But I don't aim to spook the foreman, and don't you think it.'

'Just thought I'd say,' the segundo said. 'There's just somethin' about you, that's all.' He jingled some coins in his pocket, then hitched his trousers. 'I'll let you settle in, Jack. It's time I made myself useful. I've got a gang sinking a new well out on the south range. I'd better go and make sure they haven't all drowned themselves. Okay? Anything you want before I go?'

Wells shook his head.

Rank made his way towards the door, face craning as he neared it. 'Don't starve. Ask Bill Whitty to fix you some grub, if you want. He's the cook.'

Wells gestured his understanding, then began making up his bed from the pile of blankets folded on top of its mattress. The job took him about ten minutes and didn't look much when he had finished it, but he imagined that he would sleep well enough on the bed to suit him. Then, purely for the want of something else to do, he opened up the cupboard near his bed and inspected its empty shelves, working out how and where he would place his few possessions within. After that he thought again of his horse and the meal that it was to be given, and he decided to go and see that the animal got its belly filled. Grain, to be sure. The stallion would think it was Christmas.

Walking out of the bunkhouse, Wells

made a right turn and headed for the stables. He covered the thirty yards between the buildings, then entered the equine quarters by the main door. Once beyond the threshold, he checked, peering into the hay-scented gloom before him and trying to isolate and identify shapes in his unfamiliar surroundings. He heard animals stirring on either hand, and gradually made out the positions of the aisles and stalls, advancing again as he placed where the grain bins stood on a slightly raised brick floor towards the building's back wall.

It occurred to him that his horse would need a nosebag, and he saw a number of these hanging from a hook which had been hammered into a timber roof-support towards the rear of the stables. Nearing the baulk, he was about to reach up and take down one of the bags, when his ear picked up a faint gasping from nearby and agitated movements that were interspersed with rubbing noises.

Turning to face the sounds, he gazed hard into the shadows and detected the shapes of a man and woman. The pair were propped against some bales of hay and obviously making love. The woman's hair was spilling out of the silver combs on the right side of her head, and her pale face was contorted by her passion. For the rest, there was the gleam of white flesh and glimpses of displaced garments. The two were utterly engrossed in what they were doing, and the woman's sudden outburst of ecstatic moaning told its own story.

Startled as he had seldom been, Wells watched the lovers in their now relaxing embrace for an instant longer, and was about to retreat — with the intention of leaving the stables as silently as he could and keeping the pair in ignorance of his presence — when the woman's face rolled towards him and her slowly opening eyes fixed on his own, an expression of fury and mortification coming to her beautiful features. Next moment she started whispering the fact that they had been observed into the man's ear, and his slim but massively proportioned frame began to lift off her and straighten up as he prepared to crane over his left shoulder.

Wells delayed no longer. Fearing the other's ire, he withdrew from the stables at top speed, re-entering the afternoon sunshine so abruptly that he was tempted to believe that what he had witnessed in the building at his back had not actually happened at all but been a figment of his imagination. Yet he knew better than that and, still moving at his fastest walk, headed for the corral and the spot where his horse was standing with its head thrust over the top rail of the structure's western side. He felt peculiarly sick at the stomach, for he was disgusted with himself over what he had seen. A Peeping Tom he abominated, and had never intended to become one himself. He feared also that he knew the woman's identity, and felt an intuitive certainty that he could likewise name the man. Yes, it was all a matter of intuition — and could be wrong — but he was sure that it wasn't, and cursed the evil fortune which had caused him to stumble onto such a contemptible secret during his first hour on the Broken S. If indeed secret it was. For you could never be certain about these things.

Reaching his horse, he leaned on the poles of the corral and gave the beast's neck a distracted pat, listening intently as he did so; and, within the minute, he heard footfalls approaching at his back and suddenly felt the peremptory tap of a fingertip on the top of his right arm. Turning, he found himself face to face with a good-looking, brown-haired man, who stood even taller than his own six-feet two-inches and was certainly of a much heavier build. 'What are you doing on this ranch?' the big man demanded.

'Fixing to work. Name of John Wells.'

'Figured it would be you,' the other rasped. 'So you are that Army scout Amos Spearman is forever raving about.'

'Ex-Army scout,' Wells corrected. 'You got it in one. Let's see if I can do the same. Phil Baker?'

'That's me.'

'Well, Mr Baker?'

'Mrs Spearman wants to see you.'

Wells sighed inwardly. He had surely put his foot in it! The foreman was literally bridling. This had the makings of a dangerous situation. But, as an employee, he could refuse little that was asked of him, and certainly not this. 'Very well, Mr Baker,' he said. 'Take me to her.'

3

Wells found himself walking in the direction of the ranch house again. He felt slightly dwarfed by the man beside him, though he matched Baker step for step. Jaws clenched and nostrils flaring, the foreman glared straight ahead of him, knuckles punching the air as he strode along with his arms tucked in, and Wells felt in his bones that what had just happened was not going to pass without violence. A fight of any sort was the last thing he wanted — especially as he had a normal sympathy with the other's feelings — but he had no intention of just standing there abjectly, when the storm broke, and letting Baker work him perhaps mortal harm.

They passed the northern doorway by which Amos Spearman had re-entered his home some time ago; then, coming to the angle of the house beyond it, turned left and walked along the back wall of the house, entering a bay in the brickwork which was not overlooked by windows above or on either hand. Here, without warning, Baker twisted towards Wells and, seizing him by the front of his shirt, slammed him against the wall adjacent and snarled: 'You dirty man! Is watching how you get what you need?'

'Listen,' Wells answered stonily. 'I apologise for that. It happened quite by accident. I'd received the general's permission to take grain from the stables and give my horse a feed. I happened to light on you and the lady, that's all. Don't try to tell me that nothing like it has ever happened to you.'

'That's not the point!' Baker seethed, shaking Wells hard and banging his shoulder-blades twice more against the brickwork. 'A lady's reputation has been compromised!'

'Let me go!' Wells urged. 'I've told you how it happened, and you've heard nothing but the truth. The lady's reputation won't be damaged by me. I'd rather choke than tell what I saw.'

'I'm going to make sure that you never talk about it,' Baker grated, dropping his right fist and rifling a short but very powerful punch into Wells' solar plexus.

Wells met the blow with stomach muscles braced. He absorbed it without going down, but knew that if he had not been ready for the punch, it would have sapped all the fight out of him in one go and left him helpless. 'No more!' he gasped.

'Hell!' Baker raged, setting himself to strike again.

Infuriated by the foreman's unrelenting spite, Wells knocked aside Baker's still gripping left hand and let the big man have a belly punch which carried a similar force to the one that he had himself received. His knuckles landed no less truly than the foreman's had done, but with the difference that Baker had not been prepared for what was coming. The big man caved in before the blow and, as his body let out air explosively, his knees gave way partially and his hands fell limply at his sides. This brought his unprotected jaw down to just the right level. Wells hooked for the chin with his left, then followed up with a right uppercut. Baker promptly collapsed onto his backside, legs clumsily spread and arms propping at the rear, and surprise showed through the dazed expression on his suddenly bloodied features.

The big man began to struggle erect. Wells could see at once from the set of the fellow's head and the twitching of his biceps that there was still plenty of fight left in him. Fearing that this might end in a real battle, with shocking changes to the appearances on both sides, Wells decided to do all in his power to conclude matters while he still had the advantage. Thus he wound himself up and unleashed a right cross into which he put all his weight and strength, and the blow detonated on the foreman's jaw at the spot where most damage was to be done. Down went Baker for the second time, and he lay senseless when he hit the ground, though his moments of actual unconsciousness were brief and he soon came to himself once more and forced himself into a sitting position.

He blinked up at Wells, but seemed to have no immediate idea of where he was or what had happened. But then it all appeared to come back to him with a rush and, bloody mouth gaping in a bestial snarl, he grabbed for his gun; yet the weapon had hardly begun to leave its holster, when Wells plucked out his Colt and jabbed it between the foreman's eyes, thumbing back the hammer as he softly warned: 'No, Baker. Violence has been my business for a long time. I'm very good at it. I've had to be. So just you start behaving like the ramrod of this ranch ought to. You're the man in charge, and I'll obey you on the job — same as all the other hands do — but don't you ever give me cause to pull a gun on you again. If I have to do that, I'll kill you. And do it remembering the face of a little girl that you left fatherless this day.'

'G'damn you, Wells!' Baker rubbered out, his face emptied of its earlier anger and self-righteousness and his hands lying limply between his thighs.

'As to that,' Wells said grimly, judging it safe to put up his gun, 'I reckon He probably will. But just you bear in mind what I told you. I meant every word of it.'

Baker looked at the ground and said nothing. He was certainly impressed, and he might even have been afraid. Then he lifted a hand, stretching it towards the man who had felled him. Gripping the hand, Wells pulled hard, helping Baker back to his feet, then said conversationally: 'You okay? You could do with a wash. We can delay entering the lady's presence if you want.'

'I'm fine,' Baker said shortly, giving

his jaw a wrench and dashing the blood from his lips. 'Don't talk of any more delay. You don't know the lady.'

'I guess I don't,' Wells admitted.

'Don't expect her to be ashamed of anything.'

'I won't.'

'All right then,' Baker said, heading once more in the direction they had been walking when he had cut up rough.

Wells followed the foreman now. He imagined from the other's wobbly steps that Baker felt as if he were treading on feathers. They rounded the southern end of the house. Here they approached a wooden annexe which had clearly been built in the recent past. Moving towards the further end of the additional structure, they came to a door, and Baker opened this and gestured for his companion to pursue him into the transverse passage beyond. Then, a pace or two more, and they stopped before a door centrally placed in the wall on their right. Squaring his upper body to get the best out of his unquestionably bruised and dusty appearance, Baker knocked lightly on the woodwork.

'Phil?' a woman's voice asked from behind the door.

'Yes, Madeleine.'

'Come in.'

Baker opened the door. He signed for his companion to precede him into the room beyond. Wells crossed the threshold and found himself in an office that had no great depth but crossed the full width of the annexe. Directly opposite the way in, and flanked by a pair of straight-backed chairs, stood an oaken desk, and behind the desk, lounging elegantly on a padded seat, he beheld the raven-haired woman whom he had recently seen surrendered to the foreman's embrace. No mark of that encounter showed upon her now. Her hair was all back in place, and her cheeks carried a normal colour. Not a single straw defaced the blue velvet of her gown, and the lace of her petticoats were discreetly hidden. In fact her appearance was virginal and, if the lurking wickedness in her hazel eyes were discounted, she could well have played the complete stranger to human passion. 'Here he is,' Baker said from behind Wells'back.

The woman gathered herself, then bowed forward a trifle and consulted a sheet of paper which lay on the desk before her. 'John Wells?'

'Yes, ma'am.'

'Do you know who I am?'

'I presume you to be the general's wife.'

'Yes, I'm Mrs Spearman,' she agreed, looking past Wells and letting a cruel amusement enter her gaze as she took in Baker's presence. 'Is that blood on your mouth, Phil? Did you walk into something?'

Baker moved up until he stood even with Wells, but had no ready excuse.

'He collided with a wall, ma'am,' Wells explained, hurrying to the big man's rescue. 'He had a bad fall. I had to help him up.'

'How very kind of you, Wells,' the woman said dryly. 'You really must watch what you're doing, Phil. You have a tendency to be excitable.'

'Yes, Madel — ' Baker began; but checked when he saw that her expression had changed and went to the formal and certainly more respectful: 'Yes, ma'am.'

'I might say you took me by force, Phil.'

'He wouldn't believe you,' Baker said.

'Would you believe me, Wells?' the woman asked.

'I know what I saw,' Wells answered.

'And you know the harm you could do.'

'Yes, Mrs Spearman,' Wells acknowledged. 'But where would be the sense? All I want to do is forget what I saw. And I will — if you two will let me.'

'There must have been women in your life,' Madeleine Spearman observed, eye and voice betraying female curiosity. 'Or don't sheriffs make love?'

'They love, ma'am,' Wells returned, stressing the difference.

'In the case of John Wells?'

'He's loved.'

'And made love?'

'I'm no better than the next guy. I've no right to sit in judgment on anybody.'

'I'm sure you haven't,' Mrs Spearman agreed. 'You're a sagacious fellow.'

'And you're an educated woman,' Wells said, shooting a sidelong glance at Baker. 'He doesn't know what it means either.'

'Perhaps that's just as well,' the woman said, chuckling. 'A compliment to one man too often reflects the lack in another. I feel safe with you, John Wells.'

'You are safe with me.'

'We'd better be,' Baker growled.

Wells raised an eyebrow. The man was recovering his confidence and again speaking for effect. But he imagined

Madeleine Spearman had more sense than to be influenced by it. She struck Wells as a first rate judge of character, and sharp with it. But then she surprised him by denying the gauge that he had awarded and stumbling into error. 'You heard him, Wells. We had better be.'

'Ma'am,' he responded coldly, 'I trust and hope to be trusted.'

Her eyes shifted. She had made a mistake in her handling of him, and realized it. Yet it was also plain that she did not feel able to attempt to correct her error. The echo of the higher grade person had proved false. Or was it that she had felt it necessary to lower herself into a workaday expression of loyalty to the ranch foreman — to confirm the level of duplicity to which she had committed herself? 'If you betray us,' she said, 'I'll leave you dead. The unfaithful wife of an ageing husband I may be, but I'm also a woman who never breaks her word.'

'What would you call marriage vows?'

Wells asked. 'That ageing man is still to be honoured.'

Madeleine Spearman's eyes blazed. 'Baker!'

'Shut up, Wells!' the foreman snapped. 'That's an order — ranch style!'

'I was pushed,' Wells reminded. 'If Mrs Spearman has nothing more to say — '

'I do have something more,' the dark woman snapped. 'Wells, you're a man with an over-frank tongue. I'm far from sure that men who regard themselves as trustworthy are always the right ones to trust. We'll test your true mettle tomorrow. Where it matters. Out among the thieves who have stolen our range. There could be fighting. The Enderbys — that's the father, Jake, and his two sons, Les and Sam — have shown a certain amount of backbone. I think they believe in their land grant enough to risk their lives for it. They may have help too, on the south grass. Charlie Madison and Ben Farrell may have found the courage to join the Enderbys against us. We have a report that those three families have been keeping vigil on Beacon Ridge. How does that sound to you? Does it make you afraid?'

'It's what I came up here to confront,' Wells retorted. 'I keep getting fed the rights and wrongs of it. I'll find out whether or not I can stomach the diet when the time comes. But I don't think I shall disappoint you — or myself.'

'You'll be fired if you do,' Baker said. 'That's the rule, and it applies to every one of us.'

'I guess it's about right,' Wells admitted. 'Yet I'm surprised the general made it.'

'I helped him,' the woman said, pointing at the door. 'You can go, Wells. But I want you to stay, Phil.'

Wells lifted a finger to his forelock. Then, facing about, he left the office and the annexe also, retracing the route that he had walked with Baker a short while ago and coming again to the ground on which the stables and bunkhouse were situated. He halted in the shadow of the former building, somewhat at a loose end — but thoughtful for all that, since he now believed that he had the measure of the Broken S. Amos Spearman was the boss, yet it was probably his wife who gave the orders that mattered. It was a curious set up and no mistake; and even an unlikely one where a 'strong' man like the general was involved. But it might be that Spearman was so close to what was happening that he could not see the wood for the trees. Where love was concerned, there was no fool like an old fool, and it could prove that Amos took a certain pride in his young wife's arrogance and force of character. What Wells could not believe was that Spearman had any inkling of what was going on between Madeleine and Phil Baker. That was something he must never find out — unless he discovered it for himself — since, this way or that, Wells deemed that the knowledge would cost the general his life.

Arms set akimbo, Wells looked around him. All at once he felt very much alone. There wasn't a man in sight, and a faint chill seemed to have descended on the ranch yard. The light at his back brightened, and the shadows blackened and thrust long. To the east of him, the land wore funereal hues and reached into haze: a vast emptiness beyond the arc of buildings which enclosed that section of the ranch yard. Then, abruptly conscious that he must have missed it before, he saw movement against the face of flying light and perceived a rider coming in off the grass out there and making for the gap between a barn and tool shed opposite him on the other side of the home ground.

By degrees, it occurred to Wells that the horseman was sitting his mount in the sloppiest of manners and for a time he thought the fellow drunk; but, as the other drew closer and he sensed the weakness present in his reeling posture, he realized that the rider was hurt and began moving towards the gap in the buildings to the east of him through which he believed the horseman was going to enter the ranch yard, though he caught himself again in mid-stride as he judged that the other would make it this far and that there was really no point in rushing to bring help where the need was not absolute.

Aware that the rider had spotted his presence and was now heading directly for him, Wells stood his ground, and a minute or two later the man came bumping and lurching into near focus. It was then Wells saw that the fellow's shirt had a large bloodstain over the left breast and that the other appeared to have been shot. The rider's washed-out blue eyes, now sunk back into his bony skull, told that he was suffering greatly, and his thin lips opened on tobacco-stained teeth as he tried to say something, but the effort was too much and he plunged over his mount's right shoulder and turned a half-somersault before coming to rest on his stomach.

Wells ran to the man. Crouching over him, he turned the fellow onto his back and found himself looking into those pain-filled eyes again. 'You've been in the wars, friend,' he commented.

'I don't know — you,' the wounded man complained.

'I'm a new man,' Wells explained, giving his name. 'What's your moniker?'

'Ed Lansey.'

'How'd you get in this state, Ed? Who plugged you?'

'Phil Baker sent me to — to keep an eye on — on Beacon Ridge.'

'I've heard about that spot,' Wells said, 'and the Enderbys and Farrell and Madison.'

'One o' them bastards shot me,' Lansey gulped. 'I was ridin' along, nice as you please, when bang — and I went all weak and — and I haven't been able to feel much or see right ever since. I nigh fell off my hoss twice, but he — he got me back here.'

'Are you certain it was a nester who shot you?' Wells inquired, filled with an increasing sense of dismay that he was only analysing with the top of his mind just then.

'Who else could it've been?' Lansey choked. 'Ain't but us and them nesters for miles.'

'I suppose,' Wells allowed, shaking his head sadly. 'I can't leave you lying there like that.' He looked up and all around him, but there was still nobody to be seen in the vicinity. 'I'm going to lift you and carry you into the bunkhouse.' He suited action to his words, but had no sooner got the wounded man off the ground than Lansey let out a thin scream of pain and he was forced to lower him again. 'That won't do, Ed. I'll have to go and find somebody to help me. Just you grit your teeth and hold on.'

Lansey did not answer. His eyes had closed, and it was obvious that he had lost consciousness.

Wells drew himself erect. He wasn't too sure of where to go for the best. With his almost non-existent knowledge of the ranch and how its labour was disposed, he didn't see what else he could do but run to the ranch office and seek help there, for he felt reasonably sure that he would still find Phil Baker with Mrs Spearman. Facing round, he broke into a trot and angled across the front of the ranch house, making for the eastern side of the annexe on this occasion and a door there which he had glimpsed at the opposite end of the transverse passage by which Baker and he had entered the new building during his earlier visit.

He was within a dozen yards of the annexe, and had started putting together what he was going to say, when the door ahead of him opened and Mrs Spearman emerged from it, closely followed by Phil Baker. Unsmiling, the pair were surrounded by a stormy atmosphere and Wells was certain that they had been quarrelling as they both frowned in his direction and Baker snapped: 'Now what's up with you?'

'It's not me,' Wells replied, bringing

himself to a halt. 'It's a guy named Lansey. He just rode into the yard and fell off his horse. Somebody's put a slug in him.'

Baker swore, without so much as begging the lady's pardon. 'How bad is it?'

'Mortal bad, I'd say.'

'Where is he?'

'Round by the corral.'

Baker left Madeleine Spearman and broke into a run. Pelting across the front of the ranch house, he bore right and clapped on still more pace. Taking the deepest breath that his already pumping lungs would allow, Wells turned again and began to pursue the man, coming once more to the spot where Lansey lay perhaps half a minute after the foreman had arrived.

Baker was already crouched beside the wounded man and seemed to have made a rough examination of him, for he glanced up at Wells across his left shoulder and said: 'I'm afraid you're right. This man is going home.'

'Let's get him into the bunkhouse,' Wells said.

'We can make him comfortable,' Baker sighed, 'and that's about all. Take his feet.'

Wells took hold of Lansey's ankles, while Baker got his hands under the man's shoulders. Wells straightened, and the foreman did likewise; then, with Lansey sagging between them, they began sidling towards the bunkhouse. Mrs Spearman joined them when they were about half-way there, face inscrutable — though her eyes seemed to question almost fearfully during the single moment that they met Baker's — and she stayed with them as they entered the bunkhouse and then placed Lansey on the first bed to the right of the entrance.

The foreman eased his back then, shaking his head, started a new examination, which was perfunctory in essence and appeared to be carried out mainly for the benefit of the watching female.

'I'll find somebody to ride into Amarillo,' she said suddenly, 'and ask Doctor Cotton to come out here as quickly as he can.'

'No need,' Baker said laconically, removing his right hand from the middle of Lansey's chest. 'His heart just stopped beating.'

Wells glanced quickly at Madeleine Spearman. He could have sworn that he surprised a look of relief on her face. Then, her tones noticeably theatrical, she declared: 'Somebody is going to pay for this!'

'I had detailed him to keep an eye on Beacon Ridge,' Baker said. 'This has to be the work of one of those nesters over on the south grass. You were there when he fell off his horse, Wells?'

'Yes.'

'Did you have any speech with him?'

'He told me more-or-less what you just said,' Wells answered. 'He believed one of the nesters had shot him. There was nothing more.'

'What else could there have been?' Baker queried.

Somehow it seemed a question too many. Wells studied the foreman for a moment — aware that Mrs Spearman was again looking tense as she did the same — and then shrugged his shoulders.

'The law has to be informed of this,' the woman said. 'You'd better ride into Amarillo, Phil, and tell Sheriff Boyle what's happened to Ed Lansey.'

'I'll do that now,' Baker said. 'Cover him up, Wells. I'll have our carpenter knock up a coffin for him. He'll have to be freighted into town for proper burial.'

'Uh, huh,' Wells grunted thoughtfully. 'All helps make your side of it look better.'

'You bet,' Baker agreed self-righteously. 'The folk in town know how sore vexed we've been by these damned Yankee settlers. The more they're on our side, the better for us.'

'Will you mention Bill Hastings while

you're about it?' Wells asked.

'What for?' Baker demanded.

'He's dead, too, isn't he?'

'Forget about him,' Baker commanded. 'No concern of yours.'

'None whatsoever!' Madeleine Spearman hastened. 'He had no place in your business here. Don't let his name pass your lips again.'

'That's a peculiar order, ma'am,' Wells said. 'I may have to say something before all is done. You know how one thing leads to another and they all draw together.'

'You heard me!' the woman snapped. 'Now do what the foreman told you.'

Wells inclined his head. He needed a blanket with which to shroud the body, and thought it unwise to take one from any bed nearby — for all sorts of obvious reasons — so he walked down the length of the dormitory to his own bed and removed the top blanket, returning with it, as Mrs Spearman and Phil Baker withdrew from the bunkhouse, and covering the remains

74

as he listened to the footfalls of the pair receding in the direction of the house.

The shrouding done, Wells lifted his head and stared at the wall before him. Baker and the dark woman were as jumpy as cats. He'd swear they were involved in more than an illicit love affair. He only hoped that it wasn't what he feared it could be. The situation was bad enough now without making it worse. For nothing enraged a ranch crew more than the murder of one of their number. Your average cowhand was a good-hearted fellow, but he could be equally hard when he saw the need. The death of Ed Lansey — regardless of any doubts as to how it might have come about — could put the men of the Broken S in the right frame of mind for a lynching.

Feeling more than a little frayed by his day so far, Wells sauntered back into the open and fretfully kicked his heels around the ranch yard for the next fifteen minutes. Then, as he judged the end of the working day not far off, he saw another lone rider coming in off the grass — only this man was approaching from the west, as opposed to the mortally wounded Lansey's east, and Wells had no reason to associate the pair in any way whatsoever until it struck him that there was something vaguely familiar about the manner in which the smallish, hard-faced horseman carried his head and shoulders.

Backing up against the corral rails, Wells raised a heel and spread himself into an indolent pose, watching as the other entered the ranch yard through the space between stables and bunkhouse. He made no attempt to dissemble or ignore the rider's piercing glance in his direction and, as the newcomer dismounted and tied his horse at the hitching rail outside the crew's qaurters, Wells deliberately pushed himself back into motion and began a slow advance on the bunkhouse, confirming with himself his final identification of those fierce, humourless features across the way.

It was Jack Straw, the West's number one assassin. He hadn't seen the man in several years before today. But it was Straw okay. The deadly rifleman came and went like a wraith, always leaving death behind him, and the fact of his presence was enough in itself to convince Wells that Mrs Spearman and Phil Baker had been taking active steps to make a bad situation worse.

4

Hanging back a bit, Wells watched Straw walk into the bunkhouse. He noticed that the hired killer's movements were invested with the familiarity of one who had been around the premises for some time. Any kind of settled life was foreign to Straw's reputation, so it figured that he must have been offered high pay to exercise his bloody talents hereabouts, and that was yet another grim reflection on the ruling minds of the Broken S. Wells felt increasingly depressed by it all; yet when you lived in an atmosphere of evil, all judgments had to be tempered with an allowance for that taint.

Wells decided to enter the bunkhouse without more ado, for he had the sudden feeling that Straw had recognised him as readily as he had recognised Straw. He saw no sense in behaving warily about the man. Quite the reverse in fact. Keeping his distance would only create uneasiness and suspicion between them. The more ready he showed himself to fraternise at the start, the less likely it was that any animosity would flare between them later on. After all, he, too, was a hired gun now, and that must bring him down to Straw's level, a circumstance that should accord him a certain merit in the killer's inverted estimation.

Re-entering the crew's quarters, Wells saw Jack Straw sitting on the bed beyond that on which the covered body of Ed Lansey lay. Straw was gazing speculatively at the shrouded figure, a ragged cigarette hanging unlighted from his lower lip. 'What is that?' he asked.

'What does it look like?' Wells yawned.

'A dead body.'

'There you are. Ed Lansey.'

Straw raised his right buttock a few inches, then he ripped the head of a match against his canvas seat and lifted the flame resultant to his cigarette, lighting up in a tiny flare of loose tobacco. His first inhalation was a very deep one. 'Don't surprise me,' he announced, thinned smoke pouring from his nostrils and mouth. 'Don't surprise me one bit. I heard Baker order him over to Beacon Ridge first thing this morning. Them nesters have been workin' up to it. I figured a gun would be heard before long.' He inhaled again. 'Dead, eh? Poor bastard. That sure has put a rip in it!'

'Baker's gone to report it to the law in Amarillo,' Wells said.

Straw chuckled cynically. 'Ain't that crafty? Sheriff Matt Boyle long ago declared the Broken S outside his bailiwick. I reckon our Madeleine is puttin' on the style. It'll smell that much sweeter when the Federal Law comes riding into it.'

'You think it will?'

'Only a matter of time,' Straw replied. 'I've heard tell of letters flying

80

about. But why are you asking such a question? The last time we crossed trails, you wore a tin star. You know how it all goes on.' He studied his partially smoked cigarette with dislike. 'Down El Paso way, wasn't it?'

'Crowbank.'

'Some one-horse town,' Straw agreed. 'Changed sides?'

'Obliging an old friend.'

'Amos Spearman,' Straw mused. 'There's been a heap of talk about that. We found us a problem — Wells.'

'That we have — Straw.'

A thousand lines flared in the unhealthy yellow skin of the killer's face, but his soulless eyes could not express the smile suggested. 'Go on. Tell me what it is. I want to talk. Been alone all day.'

'It's not so complicated,' Wells said, wondering how far this exposition was necessary to the needs of the moment, yet not wishing to offend the assassin. 'It comes to this. Does our government have the right to carve up established cattle country for the benefit of settlers?'

'And do the ranchers have the right to make their own law?'

'That's the rest of it,' Wells acknowledged. 'What's most right, or what's least wrong. What do you say, Straw?'

'You ask me when even the Texas Rangers can't agree?' Straw mocked. 'I don't know what the answer is. Look after number one, that's my motto. I'll keep on lining my pockets here — until I hear there's a riding marshal in the neighbourhood. Then I'll beat it. So will you. A hired gun is a hired gun. Makes no never-mind he was once a sheriff.'

'Don't rub it in.'

Rising from the bed on which he sat, Straw walked to the pot-bellied stove against the wall on Wells' left, opened the lid, squashed out his smoke on a hinge, then dropped the fragmented remains into the stove, closing up again with a metallic clunk. 'I'm tired,' he confessed, rubbing an eye. 'I've had a busy day.'

'Doing what?' Wells asked casually, his gaze dropping momentarily to the other's boots, which were pasted to the ankles with dried mud of a reddish-white hue.

'Cleaning up a line shack a few miles west of here,' Straw replied. 'The guy they put out there last winter must have been a dirty son-of-a-bitch.'

'You get 'em,' Wells conceded, while reflecting that Straw couldn't have left the shack in a particularly choice condition if he had been stomping around inside it with those caked boots on. 'D'you like working alone?'

Shrugging, Straw returned to the bed on which he had been seated previously and sat down again. 'I don't mind folk, but I like to do a job my own way.'

'I suppose I'm not so very different,' Wells confessed, glancing round as he heard movements at the door behind him and seeing two men who were in the act of entering, a rough wooden box — which had probably begun life as the packing case for a waggon axle — suspended between them.

Guessing what the two newcomers were about, Wells stepped aside and gave them all the room they needed, and they set the box down on the floor beside the bed on which Lansey's shrouded corpse lay and removed its lid. Then they lifted the body from its resting place and lowered it into the makeshift coffin, the smaller and older of the pair taking a hammer and several nails from the big pocket across the front of his carpenter's apron and starting in on the securing job without pause. And, when the lid had been tightly nailed down, he straightened up and put his hammer away, frowning at Straw and Wells. 'You guys got nothin' to do?'

'No,' Straw responded, a just detectable note of challenge in his voice.

'Some has it good,' the carpenter observed. 'Well, we can't all be lucky.

Okay, Billson — to you!'

The chunky, fat-faced Billson lifted his end of the box, as his companion raised the other, and then the two men carried their burden out of the bunkhouse and passed from sight.

Leaning forward, Straw smoothed a crease out of the top blanket of the bed from which the corpse had been removed. 'Ivor Forsyte,' he said rather maliciously, 'won't be all that happy when he hears that Ed Lansey's body lay on his bedding for a time.'

'So don't tell him,' Wells advised.

'Where'd that bullet lie?'

Wells blinked. It was a callous sort of question, but just the kind that a man who lived by his marksmanship might ask. 'High on the left side of his chest, and not too far from the heart.'

'Amazing,' Straw mused, 'how he got back here, hurt like that.'

Wells felt the promptings of instinct. He knew then Lansey's death had been Straw's work. The fact that the hired killer had ridden home out of the west meant nothing. It was easy to travel in a circle through open country. Yes, Wells knew — but could prove nothing. Yet he did have something to go on. For he had not actually told Straw that Lansey had ridden home with the bullet in him. The man could have been picked up on the range by a waggon, or even brought home over his saddle. Sure, Straw's comment could be described as a 'reasonable assumption', yet the hired gun had spoken as if certain. It was surprising to realize that Straw could be so loose in the tongue. But perhaps the fellow didn't care about giving himself away. After all, he and Wells were on the same side, and whatever he might have done would be no more than part of the larger plan to rid the Broken S of its enemies. The thought made Wells shudder now. He found it hard to credit that he had placed himself in a position where he felt obliged to acquiesce in cold-blooded murder for the sake of Spearman's grass.

'I'm going to get some grub,' Straw announced, shoving himself to his feet again. 'Are you coming? The boys will be riding in from work shortly. If we get our chow ahead of them, it'll save jostling like pigs at the trough.'

Straw led the way to a connecting door at the northern end of the dormitory. Opening it, he passed through into the next part of the building. Wells followed the assassin. He found himself in the crew's mess hall. Straw still leading, they walked to the kitchen serving hatch, where the hatchet-faced cook was just scratching the menu on the slate that hung above his range. Bacon pie, with potatoes and gravy; then lemon tart. It looked good to Wells, but brought forth only a scowl from Straw. However, bacon pie and lemon tart it had to be, and it wasn't long before they withdrew from the serving hatch, wooden trays in hand, and sat down at one of the tables nearby. For the next twenty minutes they made a leisurely meal of it, and had just finished eating, when the sound of numerous horses beating their way across the ranch yard told that the hands were now returning from the labours of the day.

Instinctively, Wells began to rise.

'Sit,' Straw urged, taking out the 'makings' and starting to roll himself a cigarette. 'We might as well have a chinwag in here as go back into that blamed sleeping place.'

Acquiescing, Wells folded his arms and watched Straw build and start smoking his cigarette. He wondered what the man's soul looked like and, if all that had been whispered about him were true, how he managed to live with his conscience. Then bellowing, energetic men burst in from the dog-trot. They filled the air with their coarse merriment, and their endless string of demands set the cook swearing like a trooper and advising them what they could do with themselves, each and every one.

'Ain't a bad bunch of boys,' Straw

said complacently. 'You can always 'buffalo' a couple if they keep it up too long.'

'Could come to that,' Wells said, grinning as he ducked to avoid a flying elbow; and he was beginning to study faces, in the hope that there might be one or two around that he had seen before, when a thudding noise called his attention to the door and he saw Phil Baker standing there and belabouring a partition on the left of the entrance with his clenched fist.

'Hey, Phil!' somebody called, as silence began settling. 'Can't we even eat in peace now?'

'No,' the foreman responded shortly, and he wasn't joking either. Indeed, his face looked grim. 'Sharp, Rearden, Colley, Bloom!' he went on. 'Straw, Adams, Wells! Get your butts out into the yard! And I do mean pronto!'

'Old Phil's got the Kruschens,' Straw remarked. 'Let's go, Wells.'

Heaving off his seat, Wells followed Straw out of the mess hall and into the ranch yard, conscious of other men striding along in his wake; and they all put the dog-trot behind them — Baker beckoning — and had moved thirty yards clear of the bunkhouse before the foreman brought them to a halt and gestured for them to gather round him. 'It's the general, boys,' he said. 'He's fit to be tied. It's because of what happened to Ed Lansey. Most of you may not know it yet, but the Beacon Ridge nesters shot and killed Ed today.

'Mrs Spearman sent me to Amarillo earlier on to report the killing to Sheriff Boyle. I only got back a short while ago, but I was summoned to Amos Spearman straightaway and he bit chunks out of me. He reckoned I should have organised immediate retaliation and to blazes with notifying the law.

'It comes to this, boys. While I'd have left settling with that murdering scum on the south grass until tomorrow, the boss insists we do it right now. He says there's still enough daylight left, and he wants you men — hired especially for the part — to drive those nesters off the Broken S before night comes and to destroy their homes and everything they possess. They're to be left with no more than the clothing on their backs.' The foreman glared around him, almost daring anybody to speak. 'Any questions? Anybody got anything to say? If there's anything you aren't sure about, let's hear it now. Only make it snappy. You may be sure the master is watching us from the house.'

'Just drive them off the land, Phil?' a hulking fellow of forty or so asked insidiously, his eye leery and his chin seeming to drip whiskers as he mangled his chaw. 'An eye for an eye, and a tooth for a tooth. Ain't it so written? It's time we got the rope out.'

'No killing!' Baker retorted. 'Furious as he is, the boss doesn't want any killing. We're to do exactly as I've told you, and no more.' His mouth gave a knowing twist. 'Of course, if shooting starts, what we may have to do in self-defence is another matter. But we mustn't be the ones to start in with pistols. Our job is to drive out and then burn.'

'I reckon that's clear enough, Colley,' said a second very large man to the one who had asked the original question. 'If you have any difficulty — '

'Leave off chipping him, Rearden!' Baker ordered impatiently. 'Any more?'

Heads were shaken all round.

'Get your horses,' Baker snapped.

Most of the men present ran back to the bunkhouse hitching rail, where their horses were tied, but Wells and Baker had to go further afield for their mounts. Wells trotted in the direction of the corral, while the foreman strode towards the house. Coming to the big enclosure, Wells lowered its drop-rail and went inside after his stallion. He caught the buckskin with a minimum of difficulty, and led it out of the corral; then, with the drop-pole back in place again, he lifted into his saddle and gigged his horse slowly eastwards, swinging right as he cleared the corral and increasing pace as the ranch party, with Baker sitting a large black gelding at its head, crossed the ground before him. Tacking on at the party's rear, he then followed the lead out of the ranch yard and onto the eastern grass, where the foreman made a ninety degree change of course and the mounts set their noses towards the rolling prairie of the south.

Baker called for a gallop. Wells kicked at his mount as the men before him did the same. Hooves rumbled and equine muscles strained. For the next fifteen minutes the ranch party travelled fast. Then a rise of some magnitude appeared blackly on the ground ahead and Wells judged from the increased tension among his companions that they were now approaching Beacon Ridge.

Glass winked momentarily on top of the height. As Wells had anticipated from all that had happened previously, the nesters in this quarter were still on watch. Somebody up there had a telescope. If he had read everything incorrectly — and the nesters had shot Ed Lansey after all and were ready to kill again — the party would soon be in range of whatever number of long-barrelled weapons happened to be present and the bullets could start to fly. His life might be on the line at any moment now.

The glass flashed again, picking up the sun's flattening light from the right, and Wells made out movement on the ridge as several figures rose from beneath the land and clustered there, obviously in urgent conference. Baker signalled for the ranch party to slow down, and a few moments later he called a halt. The men from the Broken S hunched forward in their saddles and watched the knot of figures on the ridge, while the horses snorted and tossed their heads impatiently. A sudden uncertainty seemed to have come upon everything, and Baker appeared more affected by it than everybody else.

'So they know we're here, Phil,' called the big man named Rearden. 'What can we do but attack? That's what we're here for, ain't we?'

'So it is,' Baker acknowledged, indicating a fairly wide band of obviously marshy ground that ran along the foot of the ridge before them. 'But you don't attack an enemy across a swale. That's plain asking to get bogged down. And you don't try galloping uphill from the flanks into the muzzles of waiting rifles. That's plain suicide.'

'The homesteads are on the other side of the ridge,' Rearden commented. 'Shouldn't be hard to ride round back o' Beacon and do the burning before Enderby and the others can do much about it.'

'It's always risky leaving guns at your back, Ben,' the foreman said judiciously. 'For all that we know, those hoe-men may have horses up there with them. We don't want to get charged from the rear either.'

It was the other big man, Colley, who took up Rearden's original theme now. 'We can't just sit here, Phil. We gotta get at it. This is a gun job, and well you know it.'

'Don't tell me what I know, Sam,' Baker warned. 'I've told you what our orders are. It's not only the nesters I've got to think about. It's you men as well. One Broken S funeral will be enough.' He lifted out of his saddle and peered hard at the figures on top of the ridge. 'What the hell *are* they going on about up there?'

'Maybe we should ask 'em,' Rearden said, tongue clearly in cheek.

'You're getting better, Ben,' Baker said dryly; yet he seemed to act on the advice, for he signalled a new advance and only checked again as the party neared the edge of the swale and a voice called to them off the height.

'What's that?' Baker demanded.

'We don't want trouble,' came the answer.

'You got it!' the foreman answered. 'In Spades!'

'We didn't kill that man of yours.'

'Who is that?'

'Jake Enderby.'

'General Spearman wants you off his land right now, mister, and we're going to put you off!'

'I say, we didn't kill that man of yours, Mr Baker.'

'We say you did, Enderby!'

'It was somebody else!' Enderby protested. 'One of your men, we reckon. We saw him sneak out of a fold and ride off northwards.'

'Tell me another!' Baker scorned.

'I'm comin' down to talk!'

'You do,' Baker cautioned, 'and we'll have the hide off you!'

'I'm comin' down to talk!' Enderby repeated; and the man, a lean, stooped figure, separated from his companions on the summit above and started descending that slope in front of the ridge at a checked run.

'He's as stupid as you are, Rearden!' the foreman threw back across his right shoulder, reaching under the flap of his saddlebag on that side and drawing out a coiled stock-whip that was tipped with lead. 'I warned him, boys! You all heard me warn him! I'll flay him to the bone! His screams will take the heart out of that nest of skunks up there!'

Wells flinched at the vision that his mind produced, and he could not help himself as he called: 'Is that in line with Amos Spearman's orders, Baker?'

'I don't see it out of line,' Baker replied. 'Want to lay on some? We'll take it in turns, if you like.'

Although he was separated from the man by a space that contained the physical presence of six others, Wells could feel the sadism and cruelty emanating from Baker. Here, then, was the true measure of the person who had shot Bill Hastings and claimed that it had been self-defence. This incident more-or-less proved that Baker had the instincts of a beast capable of anything. Doubtless the foreman's true nature was hidden most of the time, but here the inner man was exposed in all its vileness. Wells' first instinct was to turn from this business with such dignity as he still possesed, but his loyalty to Amos Spearman and his basic doubt of the nester's case continued to hold and frustrate him. He had ridden several hundred miles to take a hand in this job, and he fully grasped that the actions necessary to it had to be ruthless and unlovely. He was indeed ready to chivvy the nesters some; but how could he go through with this? Or let anybody else do so? He had been the defender of the weak; and those people on the ridge were the weak. The poor devils had nothing. And the general had everything. God in heaven! What was he to do?

Jake Enderby had reached the bottom off the slope that formed the northern face of Beacon Ridge. Wells watched the gaunt figure, some years over sixty, come plodding and squelching across the tussocky area of the swale. A more unprepossessing old man it would have been hard to find, yet there was a certain strength in the cut of Enderby's creased and wrinkled jib which fired up the spirit of honesty that Wells had been trying to suppress in the name of those false values which paraded the blackmail of being true.

Enderby cleared the swampy ground. Chest pumping, and with moisture dribbling from the corners of his mouth, he began slowing towards the ranch party. Baker laughed at the sight. Then he shook out the plaited bullhide coils of his whip. He cracked the leaded weave with maximum force, producing a noise like a pistol shot, and leaned forward in preparation to lay on; but in the same instant Wells saw a fresh mud on the old man's boots that was thick with chalk and the reddish hue of rotting sandstone. There could be no question that it was the same mud which clung in a dried state to Jack Straw's boots. For Wells it was proof enough that Straw had bushwhacked Ed Lansey — proof enough of murder!

5

Though he kept in the background, Wells no longer had any doubt of what he must do; and he said: 'No, Baker. You hear that man out.'

Baker's head came round again, his features betraying a startled disbelief. 'What was that, Wells?' he demanded. 'Did I hear you right?'

'I said we must hear Enderby out,' Wells answered stonily. 'You keep that whip to yourself.'

'You're finished, man!' Baker declared. 'You were warned how it would be if you started trying to play the sheriff!'

'Okay, I'm finished,' Wells said flatly. 'Now hear him out.'

'Please!' begged Jake Enderby, who had now stopped beside the foreman's horse and was hanging on to its mane. 'We're honest men, Mr Baker!'

'Are you, by heck!' Baker snorted,

a note of disdainful tolerance suddenly present in his voice. 'We wouldn't have known. Very well. Say your say.'

'All we want,' Enderby gasped, clearly fighting his shortness of breath and groping for the right words, 'is to farm our government holdings and live out of whatever profits our crops bring in. We ain't touched so much as a buffalo chip belongin' to General Spearman, and we won't — ever. We'll even fence in our ground so's we don't have any contact with the cows from your herds.' The old man released the mane that he had been holding and threw up his hands. 'Lord have mercy, sir! What more can I say? My boy Les's missus is near her time. You can't put a woman in her condition out on the prairie. She'll die if you do. Sweet Jesus, Mr Baker! Her and her baby'll die!'

'I doubt it,' Baker said callously. 'The type of female who teams up with your kind is tougher than that. Anyhow, it won't matter much if her and her brat snuff it. It'll amount to two less sodbusters in a world that's already got a thousand times too many of them.' He jerked his chin. 'Colley! — Rearden! I see a thorn tree across the way. I want you to take this man to it and tie him there, face to the bark. You can rip his shirt off when you've done that. This place is going to ring with his screaming before long.'

It had reached the point at which Wells knew that he must take definite action. 'Forget it, Baker!' he warned, the torture of his soul abruptly resolved in the revelation that it was not in him to do other than the right in a moment of need. 'You may consign your own soul to the burning, but you're not consigning mine. And I don't believe these hardcases came out with you to make war on a woman in childbed. I'm good and sure the general wouldn't want it either. He'd be the first to boil water and find the swaddling clothes. If Madeleine Spearman would want it, then you and her deserve each other as much as I believe you do. Man, I despise you both!'

'Have you gone off your rocker, Wells?' the foreman inquired, his features again wearing disbelief. 'None of this is any of your business. You're fired — finished. Can't you see?'

'You make it too simple,' Wells said implacably.

'What is this about?'

'Murder,' Wells replied. 'Ed Landsey's murder by Jack Straw. You and Mrs Spearman arranged it to give yourselves a strong excuse for what's happening here.'

'You're accusing,' Baker rasped.

'I am.'

Baker dismounted. 'Get off your horse!'

Wells swung to the ground. The riders before him parted, and he stood facing the foreman.

'What's your proof?' Baker demanded.

'Look at Jack Straw's boots,' Wells responded, 'then at Jake Enderby's. It's the selfsame mud. Straw told me that he had spent the day at a line shack far west of here. There's the proof he didn't. He picked up that mud at this place, while he was laying for Lansey. What you and Mrs Spearman schemed was smart enough, Baker, but it's been done before — and less clumsily.'

The foreman looked up and to his right, eyeing Straw, who was resting on his pommel. 'Are you going to let him say these things, Jack?'

'Words,' Straw said indifferently. 'So I've got mud on my boots. He's not going to claim them as evidence. There's buffalo wallow on the west grass. What can he prove?'

'He needs killing!' Baker protested.

'So he does,' Straw agreed, shrugging, though his gaze was wicked.

'Do it, Jack,' the foreman urged. 'Do it!'

Straw chuckled and shook his head. 'That's John Wells. He's one of the true fast guns. A legend down in the border country. I ain't up to a draw-and-shoot with the likes of him. 'Taint my way anyhow. I'll kill him, Baker.

This year, next year — I'll kill him.'

'You're scared of him!' Baker sneered.

'So I am,' the hired killer admitted.

'I'm not!' Baker declared pridefully; and he went for his gun.

Wells had been sure it was coming. Had Baker's crimes been less — or his attitude different — he might have done all in his power to discourage the foreman from pulling on him; but as it was, he drew and fired in a split second, and Baker toppled backwards with his gun still not clear of its holster. He lay with his left hand thrown back behind his head and his left knee raised. A moment went by. Then his leg slowly flattened, and Baker's head rolled, the jaw settling into the hollow of his left shoulder.

Jack Straw dismounted. He walked over to the fallen man and looked down into his face. 'Dead,' he announced, glancing sideways at Wells. 'Young and foolish.'

'You might say that,' Wells acknowledged.

'Poor Madeleine,' Straw observed. 'She's going to take this hard. I wouldn't have her riled at me for worlds. I reckon she might take the right to kill you away from me. Wells, you're an unlucky man. You must be to have made two such enemies. Was I you, mister, I'd get on that horse of mine and ride.'

Wells weighed his revolver for a long moment. He looked for any indication of a threat among the riders nearby. The men were quiet in their saddles and there was nothing to suggest any immediate danger to him. 'Thank you, Straw,' he said. 'This is one time I'm going to take your advice.'

'Be seeing you,' Straw promised.

'No doubt,' Wells said, backing towards his horse; and, reaching the animal, he holstered his gun and stepped into his saddle. Then, fetching the stallion's head round, he drove in his spurs and went galloping away east of north. He feared that the mood behind him could undergo an abrupt change, and that a roll of gunfire might pursue him; but in fact no shot was detonated in his wake, and two minutes of hard riding bore him well beyond the range of any gun carried by a member of the Broken S party. Then, topping a rise, he allowed himself a quick look back — for there was also the risk of pursuit — but he saw that Straw and company were clustered about Baker's remains and that they all appeared to have lost interest in his flight.

Wells kept his mount at full gallop for perhaps another mile. After that he slowed down somewhat in order to conserve the animal's strength. It had already had a hard day, and he was afraid that he might still have to make big demands on it. Then, his thoughts moving wholly to himself, he started to consider possible futures, with safety as the first requirement of each. For just now his one desire was to travel as far from death and conflict as possible.

Oklahoma exercised the biggest draw on his mind. He estimated that he couldn't be more than seventy-five miles from the Territorial line at his present point. If he crossed over, he could dwell awhile in the relative security of Nations, but that did pose the problem of earning an honest living where most of the work to be had was of the dishonest kind. Still, he could have better luck if he kept travelling north; for he seemed to recall a recent newspaper advertisement concerning the Kansas Pacific Railroad's need for men experienced in guarding bullion and mail. Mining jobs had also been advertised by more than one northern mining company, and work of all sorts was available in the big towns along the Mississippi. Failing any of that, there was the possibility of going all the way east and seeing what he would see. Suddenly he found himself in a state of enthusiasm for almost every job in this wideflung future, and he wondered why he had been so troubled a short while ago; but then the light in his mind began to burn dimmer and the realities that lay before its glare came fully back into focus.

He found himself smiling wryly as pressure on the bit that he was almost unconscious of applying eased his mount's nose closer and closer to due east. It was time to tell himself the truth. He was playing the coward; he was running away; and that was all very well for him. But, by shooting Phil Baker, he had made trouble which others would have to suffer in his absence. For, having sensed the bitter and revengeful nature of Madeleine Spearman — and judged that total implacability went with it — he felt sure that the woman would strike out almost at once and in the most cruel and destructive of manners to get her own back. If she couldn't hurt him, it was obvious that the nesters would have to bear the brunt. With the stony heartlessness of which only a truly wicked woman was capable, she would annihilate them; and later, when the time of reckoning came, she would smile in all her beauty at the Federal Law and spin a yarn to account for the death and arson that would put her entirely in the clear. In every lie she would be backed up by her kindly and besotted husband, and once again the most heinous crimes would pass unpunished. No, he could not allow such injustice. Bucking a stacked deck though he might be, he must turn back now and play this game out, even though he saw little chance of winning.

Turning his horse through ninety degrees, he began heading southwards, and it wasn't long before he brought Beacon Ridge back into view. Now he rode with a quieter mind, though there was fear in him too. The light had flattened still further, and the sun was setting now, lakes of fire flooding about its sinking orb and fields of rich colour spreading on either side of the event and running into shadows that darkened the edges of the range. There was beauty in the hour, and Wells lifted his eyes towards it, but there was a sinister quality present too, and it came out of the east as a silent wind that chilled his spine.

As he drew nearer to Beacon Ridge, Wells became aware of a certain presumption in what he was doing. He was taking it for granted that the nesters had need of him. Supposing they told him that they were quite capable of looking after themselves and sent him on his way? The problem was theirs, and the basic situation had existed before his arrival. He had offended Madeleine Spearman, yes — and felt that he ought to set himself up as a kind of Aunt Sally because of it — but he could hardly expect the nesters to see him as a saviour and to regard his appearance with gratitude. They might even feel that he was a turncoat and not worthy of their respect or, worse still, a guy assuaging his conscience. In fact he was beginning to regard himself as a muddling, self-righteous hypocrite, who should have stuck to his law office down in Crowbank, for he could see now that he had always been kidding himself with his friendship excuses and that he had indeed left Crowbank to free himself from onerous responsibilities rather than with Amos Spearman's best interests at heart. But none of that had much relevance this evening. He was in a developing situation and could only see how it came out.

Wells kept moving in a shallow curve that should take him to the rear of Beacon Ridge. The scene levelled to the left of the darkening height, and a smoky twilight hazed the lost skyline of the south. The wind was audible now, and the bluster of it caught in his light garments. He shivered and braced himself; then turned westwards and looked down the back of the ridge, making out the black shape of a sodhouse upon the darkening land ahead, areas of broken soil before the dwelling, and the shapes of four men, hands in pockets and shoulders hunched, looking towards him from a spot near the building's rear with apathetic expressions on their pale features. No man among the four so much as stirred as he drew near, and they remained just as frozen as he rode right up to them and reined in. 'Good evening, gents,' he greeted prosaically enough.

'It is him,' said the man standing furthest to the left, in whose lank, stooped figure Wells recognised Jake Enderby. 'Okay, mister. I'm indebted to you. You saved my hide over yonder. What do you want?'

'Nothing, Mr Enderby,' Wells replied — 'in the sense I think you mean. It's what I want to offer, and that's my help.'

'Um.'

Wells frowned. The old man wasn't hostile, and he wasn't disbelieving, nor yet submissive; he simply didn't care, and carried all the signs, in tones and appearance, of one who had given up and was just waiting for the blow to fall. 'I reckon they've taken Baker's body home. You know they're going to kill you when they come back?'

'And mightn't that be your fault?' Jake Enderby asked.

'Pa!' protested one of the younger men on Enderby's left. 'You said yourself that big hellion Baker was going to whip you to shreds. Hell, suh — you said so! This man came between you and that. And you talk about fault!'

'No, boy,' Wells said quietly. 'Your pa clearly knows these people for what they are. He's right. When I shot Phil Baker, I invited something far more frightening than Amos Spearman's rule. I'm talking about his wife's revenge. Baker was her fancy man, and Madeleine Spearman is a pure bred hellcat. Before this time, the Broken S would have been content to see you people walking the grass and homeless, but now your blood will be required to pay for Phil Baker's.'

'That's it, Sam,' Jake Enderby said grimly. 'Put plain.'

'Well, I ain't blamin' you, mister,' Sam Enderby said. 'From what I saw off Beacon Ridge, you only did what you had to do — and needed doing.'

'We're of the same mind there,' Wells admitted. 'You folk ought to be preparing to defend yourselves. I wouldn't be surprised if the Broken S attacks you during the night.'

'We're at their mercy,' Jake Enderby said hopelessly. 'If it weren't for Milly — Les here, my eldest's wife, having her little 'un, we'd have made a bolt for it long ago. As it is — '

'You're not at their mercy,' Wells said angrily. 'You're at the mercy of your own fear. Nothing else. Baker died easily enough, and so will any man riding for the Broken S. You've got guns, haven't you?'

'Sure.'

'And you know how to use them?'

'Use 'em!' old man Enderby scoffed pridefully, digging at the willowy form of his son Sam. 'Sam here was champion target shot of Ohio. I'm fair-to-middlin' too; and Les ain't all that bad. But we ain't mankillers. Ain't one of us ever shot at a man.'

'There's got to be a first time,' Wells reminded. 'It should make the difference when the other guy is trying to kill you. Sounds to me like I'm in better company than I though. It's not every day you meet a champion shot.'

'You're a hard bastard!' Jake Enderby declared. 'What do you want to turn us into? We're God-fearin' men, and killin' is forbidden in the Good Book. But I guess you wouldn't know about that. You're just another o' these Texas gunmen. Been murderin' all your life, I expect.'

'I've killed several men in my time,' Wells admitted. 'But never one who didn't richly deserve it. Nor am I one of your Texas gunmen. My name is John Wells. Until a short while ago, I was the sheriff of Crowbank, a little town down in the border country.'

'Then how in tarnation did you come to get mixed up with Spearman's murder band?' asked the fourth man in Enderby's group. 'Them's in the wrong, mister, and this here's Ben Farrell a-tellin' of you. We got our government papers, sir. You've been sidin' against the law. And that's no place for a man who says he's been a sheriff to be.'

'You're right, Farrell,' Wells conceded. 'General Spearman was my commanding officer when I was an Army scout, years ago. He did me much good, and I still regard him as a friend. But I discovered an hour or so back I can't serve his cause. Not because I consider it's all wrong, any more than I regard yours as all right, but common humanity is being breached on this land and that's got to be fought. That's why I'm here to throw in with you. If you want me.'

'Safety in numbers, suh?' Jake Enderby inquired sarcastically. 'You figure you've got a better chance if you make us your army? Brazen, that's how I see it, and it don't become you.'

'You're not quite a dunderhead,

Jake,' Wells said bluntly. 'Help me, help yourself. You stand there like a row of lilies and the Broken S will most likely cut you down. Load your guns and fight 'longside me, and we may all survive. There are some tough varmints on the other side, and they roar, but gunpowder long since made all men equal on the battlefield. Pull yourself together, Jake!'

'Who d'you think you're talkin' to, young fellow?' Enderby demanded indignantly. 'If one of my two boys talked up to me like that, I'd kick his — '

'Sure you would,' Wells interrupted, 'and right too. You keep on showing spirit. It's what we need.' He gazed upwards into the dusk, conscious of a bat wobbling above the sodhouse at speed. 'Les Enderby, and Sam. You're young men. Do you want to die? Are you ready to die yet?'

'Of course we ain't!' Les Enderby snorted, birdlike in his hunched stance. 'This man's right, pa. We don't have to let ourselves be killed on account of the Good Book or anything else. I reckon our fate's in our own hands. We got rifles, and we got bullets. I vote we fort up in the sodhouse. It's got walls of best railroad ties and a packin' of turfs thick enough to absorb all but cannon balls.'

'It wouldn't burn all that easy either,' Wells remarked. 'If horsemen come galloping up with blazing torches in their hands and throw them on top of the place, the roof won't take fire. It'll be for you to shoot the riders through their briskets.'

'How about dynamite?' old Jake asked negatively. 'How do railroad ties stand against that?'

'Let's hope any attackers we see aren't carrying dynamite,' Wells retorted. 'Do you figure the Broken S would expect a hard enough battle to need that?'

'No,' Farrell chipped in. 'They'd reckon us no contest. Gotta be sane about it, Jake.'

'I'm with brother Les, pa,' Sam

Enderby said, 'and Mr Wells. Let's make a fight of it. You don't have to take part. We know you ain't young any more.'

Jake Enderby turned on Sam and soundly boxed his ears. 'I'm still a better man than you'll ever be, sprout!' he snarled. 'I can fight!'

'And you will,' Wells agreed. 'Do I stay?'

' 'Cos you do,' Farrell said.

'Step down, suh,' Jake Enderby agreed.

'I thank you,' Wells said, dismounting. 'Where do I put my horse?'

'There's grass all around,' Jake Enderby informed him, 'and good water in a spring-hole this side of yon ridge. That hoss of yours looks like he's man enough to look after himself.'

'At that,' Wells acknowledged, 'I've never known him to miss out yet.' He gave his mount a slap on the rump that sent it trotting into the gloom behind the sodhouse, where it stopped at a point at which it was still just visible and put its nose down and began to graze. 'I imagine you've left a look-out on the ridge, Mr Enderby.'

'Charlie Madison's on watch,' Jake agreed.

'What's the signal — if Spearman's gunnies reappear?'

'A whistle.'

'It's some distance,' Wells said critically.

'When Charlie Madison whistles,' Enderby said, 'they can hear him north o' Kansas City.'

'That means the enemy would hear him too,' Wells pointed out. 'It's never wise to let a foeman know you've spotted his approach. You lose the advantage of a surprise shot.'

'You leave her how she is,' the old man ordered. 'I don't aim to shoot any man but what he's first been warned.'

'I accept the morality of it,' Wells growled, 'but I'm not sure about its wisdom.'

'Leave her be!'

Wells said no more. He sensed that arguing with Jake Enderby would be the same as trying to reason with a brick wall. The important thing was indeed to know that the enemy was coming. If Charlie Madison could alert his neighbours with a whistle, good enough.

'You'd better come indoors, Wells,' old man Enderby said. 'Meet the missus and Les's wife. Nice how-d'you-do! We'll be like rats in a trap in there — if it comes to a fight — and a woman in labour too. Golly!'

'It's known as making the best of a bad job,' Wells said. 'Anything else is impossible — if you want to see another sun go down.'

Jake Enderby had already turned away. Wells followed him to the front of the sodhouse. The old man opened the door there and stepped inside. Wells ducked after him, at once conscious of an atmosphere that was too warm for comfort and thick with woodsmoke. A lantern hung from the beam which supported the middle of the turf roof, and the light from it spread dimly over the rather foul interior of the primitive dwelling. It revealed an open fire near the wall on the right and a truckle bed against that on the left. Upon the bed lay a vaguely pretty but obviously underfed young woman who had closed her eyes and was biting her left hand to stifle her cries as the contractions of childbirth came and went. A much older woman, no less thin and losing her white hair, was kneeling near the foot of the truckle and wiping away the sweat from the encouched girl's brow. 'You can see which one is Milly,' Enderby said. 'The other one's Martha, my wife, and the mother o' them two numskulls we left outside.' He gave his wife's left shoulder a rough shake, and she turned her head and looked up, revealing a face that carried the wrinkles and lines of the last season of its years. 'This is John Wells, mother.'

'Mr Wells.'

'Ma'am.'

'We're going to fight the Broken S,' Enderby explained to his wife. 'Mr Wells has come to stand with us. He's the man who saved me from Phil Baker's whip. I told you about that a while ago.'

The woman nodded. 'Be not afraid. The Lord will provide.'

'I hope so,' Wells said, eyeing the younger woman gravely. 'Does that girl need medical care?'

'I can manage,' Martha Enderby said. 'Midwifery has been my life's first duty. This ain't a good birth, Mr Wells, but I've seen far worse. First babies can be a trial for all concerned.'

'You hungry, Wells?' Jake Enderby asked, throwing coals onto the fire.

'No,' Wells answered. 'I ate a good meal not so long ago.'

'Good,' the old man said crisply. 'There ain't much here. The land's rich in game, but we ain't had the chance to go shootin' lately. There's been too much else to think about.'

'I can imagine,' Wells sighed, most of his attention still on the older woman. 'I hope you fully understand this, Mrs Enderby. This could be a mighty rough night. If it runs into tomorrow, there's still a fight coming. No help for it. There could be bullets flying about in here. Each of us will have to take his or her chance. I wish I could say something to make it sound less awful. But there's nothing. Just — nothing.'

'It's all right, Mr Wells,' the old woman said, smiling. 'Like I said. We'll be protected. The Lord knows where it's needed. Suffer little children — '

'Sure,' Wells acknowledged. 'Phew! These ladies need air, Mr Enderby. We're taking up too much of it. We don't have to pack this place before necessary.'

'Reckon we don't,' Jake Enderby agreed. 'Farrell's a bach, so we don't have to worry about family with him, but Charlie Madison has a wife. She's settin' in their cabin, half a mile west o' here, and — '

'Go and fetch her, Jake,' his wife ordered.

'Was then thinkin' about it,' Enderby replied. 'I'll go right now.'

Jake Enderby stepped outside again, closely pursued by Wells. By unspoken agreement, they checked a yard or two beyond the building — each apparently giving the other the chance to say anything that he wished to say — but neither spoke and, after studying the first stars for a moment and testing the direction of the wind, they parted, Enderby striding off westwards and Wells circling out to the east, deliberately avoiding the figures of Sam, Les, and Farrell as he made for his horse and some indefinable need of its companionship. However, missing the animal somehow — and then undergoing a slight change in mood — he walked on towards the black edge of land that silhouetted the early night sky to the north of him. The desire to meet Charlie Madison was suddenly upon him, and he began to climb the slope at the rear of Beacon Ridge, noting a shimmer of moonlight on the grass underfoot as the wind stripped the rising lunar body of cloud.

Bracing his leg muscles and digging in his heels, Wells toiled up the grade, reaching the top within two minutes and discerning on his right the shape of a man who was looking towards him. 'Jake?' the other inquired uncertainly.

'No,' Wells answered; and he gave his name and explained why he had come to the Beacon Ridge homesteads and how Jake Enderby and the others had received him, ending: 'So now we're all on the same side, I thought I'd come up and make your acquaintance. Bit crowded in Jake's place. By the way, he's gone to fetch your wife.'

'That's good,' Madison said. 'I'd hate to think she was all by herself if anything did happen.'

'Something's going to happen,' Wells assured him, looking out into the swelling miles of obscurity beyond the ridge. 'You can bet your bottom dollar on it.'

'I've felt it building,' Madison muttered. 'What did we come here for?'

'To earn a living,' Wells said. 'What's more important to a man?'

'The government's deserted us,' Madison said unhappily. 'I wish I'd stayed in Ohio. It's better country than this. I'm going back there first chance I get. Texas has no hold on me.'

'You'll feel better about it when the anxiety lifts,' Wells said. 'It will one of these days.'

'Where's the Federal Law?' Madison demanded. 'We've asked for it. There ought to have been a riding marshal here before now.'

'Who said it has to be easy?' Wells sighed. 'The law has its problems too.'

Madison grunted non-committally. He made a squat, over-broad figure as he bent forward and peered northwards with the newly filtering moonlight. 'Do I see horsemen yonder?'

Wells concentrated his gaze into the near distance. 'You do,' he confirmed. 'A real big bunch of them. It's the Broken S crew all right. Figures Madeleine Spearman sent every manjack this way after Baker's body had been delivered to her. This is where we find out what we're made of, Charlie.'

6

Wells sensed a momentary paralysis in his companion; but then Madison hooked his fingers into his mouth and prepared to whistle the alarm. More than ever convinced of the madness of warning an enemy that he had been spotted, Wells gave the look-out a slight push and said: 'Don't whistle. What's to come is too serious to let them know they've been seen. Let's run down to Enderby's place.'

Facing south, they left the ridge together. Down the slope they went, elbow to elbow, plunging recklessly. They reached the bottom in about half a minute and then stretched their legs into a run, crossing the grass between ridge and sodhouse at a pace that would have done credit to a champion foot-racer. They rounded the dwelling's western end and, approaching the front door, almost ran full butt into Les and Sam Enderby who, with Ben Farrell, had obviously moved from the eastern side of the sodhouse since Wells had seen them last. 'What gives?' Les asked tensely.

'They're coming!' Wells panted, having skidded to a halt as Madison had done the same. 'Looks like the whole Broken S crew. More than thirty guys. They'll need time to come round the ridge, but I reckon they'll be here in ten minutes.' He gasped for breath, feeling the pain of it in his throat. 'Get indoors! Make your guns ready!' Again he fought for air. 'Is your pa back yet?'

'Where'd he go?' Les Enderby asked.

'Madison's place. Half a mile, he said.'

'That's a mile there and back,' Madison himself reminded.

'He didn't go armed either,' Wells recalled. 'You go into the house with these fellows, Madison. Help protect the women in there. I'll go and see where Jake's got to.'

Les Enderby started to say something, but Wells didn't wait to hear what it was. He faced round and began running in a westerly direction. Realizing that he had set out in a rather hit-or-miss sort of manner, he hoped that he would see or hear Enderby and Mrs Madison as he left the shadow of the ridge and came again to what he expected to be completely open land, but he had to admit to himself the danger of missing the pair in the night's latest spell of almost total darkness, for the rising moon had again been obscured by cloud.

He ran at what became an increasingly steady pace for about four hundred yards. Conscious that he was beginning to lose his sense of direction, he peered around him in mounting desperation. Where in tarnation were Enderby and the woman? If he didn't locate them soon, and get them to the sodhouse in a hurry, all three of them were going to get caught in the open and end up as a mite of target shooting for Jack Straw and company. G'damn it! Where had that pair got to? They ought to have got this far by now. Yet was that so? Enderby had had no reason to believe that trouble would break as soon as it had, and he might be lingering talkatively in the Madison parlour. After all, according to the shape of events, he and the woman would have plenty to discuss.

Suddenly Wells found the temptation too much for him. 'Enderby!' he called in the lowest but most penetrating voice that he could manage. 'Enderby!'

Rather to his surprise, he got a reply from about a hundred yards ahead. 'Wells?'

'Yes.'

'What's up?'

'The Broken S — they're riding in!'

'Consarn it!'

Halted now, Wells heard footfalls moving rapidly towards his position. 'Have you got Mrs Madison with you?' he asked, doubting for an instant.

'I'm here!' a woman's voice answered.

The clouds parted, and the moon shone through, its pallid light touching Jake Enderby's labouring shape and the figure of a female who looked many years younger than her companion. 'We must get to Jake's house as fast as we can!' Wells urged. 'Spearman's riders could turn up in front of it at any moment!'

Jake Enderby and Mrs Madison drew level with Wells. He turned round and began to run with them. The moon went on shining down from a sky that had again blown clear. Enderby's sodhouse was just about visible in the shadows on the ground ahead. But coming into sight too were the riders of the Broken S. The horsemen were as yet the better part of a mile away, and stood little chance for the moment of spotting the runners on the darkened land to the south of the ridge, but they were advancing at three times the pace that Wells and company were making, and it was already obvious that it would be touch and go as to whether the riders or the people afoot arrived at the sodhouse first.

'Faster!' Wells gulped, taking Enderby and the woman by the right and left hands respectively and forcing them to the limit as he did the same to himself.

The Broken S party kept coming out of the east, and its blur of shapes became individual riders. Wells judged the remaining distance that he and the pair running with him had still to cover. It was about two hundred yards. Nothing really. Yet he was suddenly sure that the ranchmen were going to reach the vicinity of the dwelling seconds to the good, and that they must spot him and his companions before they could enter the Enderby home.

Wells released his holds on Jake Enderby and Mrs Madison. 'Keep running!' he shouted at them. Then he drew his revolver and aimed among the foremost riders in the ranch party, triggering three times and fast, and the night was split by the bellowing explosions and the horsemen checked into sudden chaos as a mount pitched onto its nose and its abruptly somersaulting master yelled his fright.

Believing he had made the seconds that he and his companions needed, Wells got his legs moving at top speed again. He saw Enderby and Mrs Madison reach the sodhouse and pass through the front door that had been opened for them by a hand unseen. He knew that hand was waiting to do as much for him, but then he felt a sinking in his stomach as he perceived that the ranchmen had made a far more rapid recovery than he had thought possible, broken ranks about the fallen horse and their sprawling comrade, and resumed their advance at a rate that was rapidly approaching full gallop.

Guns began to flash along the front line of riders. Wells heard bullets pass his head. Sure now that he had no chance of reaching the sodhouse ahead of the ranch party, he slowed up and fired twice more. Again he was lucky. A saddle emptied, and the riderless horse swung wide and created another moment of confusion among the men from the Broken S.

Knowing that he now held an empty revolver — and could not give further battle until he had made the opportunity to reload the weapon — Wells slanted to his left and, using the blackest shadows in the area, headed into the land between the southern base of Beacon Ridge and the back of the sodhouse, placing the dwelling between him and the slugs from the horsemen.

He heard a splutter of shots from the front of the sodhouse. The men inside the building had found their nerve and got into action. Thank God for that! The lead from their rifles should provide the men from the Broken S with a new worry and take their minds off him. Halting near the dwelling's rear wall, Wells broke out his loading gate and spun his reeking cylinder clean, packing shells from his gunbelt into the Colt's chambers and then closing up again, setting the pistol at full cock.

Then it occurred to him that he would be a still more deadly force with a rifle in his hands, and he remembered the Winchester on his saddle. He looked for his horse in the half-light of the gusty night, but detected no trace of the brute on the grass to his left. Had the mount bolted at the sound of guns? No, it was too well trained for that. He put on his thinking cap. Ah! He'd bet he knew where the critter was. Jake Enderby had spoken of there being a spring on this side of Beacon Ridge. The animal must have been thirsty by the time they got here; so the probability was that it had gone for a drink and was now cropping in the neighbourhood of the water.

Wells made for the ground under the slope of the ridge adjacent. The noise behind him built into a crescendo of blast and counter-blast. He got the impression that the men in the sodhouse were more than holding their own. There was dew in the grass, and it soaked his boots and chilled his feet. Where the devil was that horse? Then he shivered; but the shiver was one of apprehension rather than cold; for he suddenly heard horses moving on the ground behind him, and guessed that their riders were seeking him.

Then he saw the horse. Despite the gunfire, it was tearing at the grass placidly enough, and it hardly raised its head as he ran up and stopped beside it, shoving his Colt away and then sliding his Winchester from its sheath. Still facing the horse, he thumbed back his hammer on the shell that he knew to be in the long gun's barrel; then, startled anew as shots rattled at his back and lead scored the upper heel of his right boot, stinging like mad, he whirled round, covering the first of the three riders that he saw heading for him and pulling the trigger. His rifle kicked, and the man at whom it was aimed toppled backwards out of his saddle. Then Wells levered at his weapon and fired twice more, his shots going to left and right, and the two other horsemen who had threatened him received body wounds, the first turning away doubled over his pommel and the second disappearing, as his horse took control, with the same kind of sagging and bouncing motion as a dummy tied in place.

Remaining alert, Wells looked for other horsemen in his vicinity, but there were no more around. Then, moving at a crouched run, he headed for the rear western corner of the sodhouse and flung himself in tight against it, working his way quickly along the wall beyond it after that and coming to the front of the dwelling and a view of what was happening on the southern land. He saw horsemen manoeuvring on the grass and broken ground within the field of moonlight beyond him, and noted several riderless mounts on the fringes of the scene, which told of casualties; but the number of Broken S employees still active was considerable, and Wells didn't doubt that the men opposite had been given the order not to return to the ranch yard until the nesters at Beacon Ridge had been wiped out; which was a daunting thought.

Wells listened to the guns cracking and booming along the front wall of the sodhouse. Through the detonations, he heard voices shouting commands out on the grass. He recognised the tones of Jack Straw and Even Rank, and imagined that Straw would be in command, with Rank backing up. So far as he could be sure, Amos Spearman had kept out of this attack, and that was something of a relief, for he did not wish to see harm come to the man and honestly thought that his old commander was not the originator of the worst evils springing from the Broken S.

Then, after some half-hearted derring-do from the odd horseman here and there, Wells received the quite unexpected impression that the Broken S riders were pulling back; but, as the voices of Straw and Rank became audible again, he decided that the enemy was regrouping for an all-out charge. There was a brief lull, and then this was confirmed by a rumbling of hooves and a fearful yelling. Wells soon made out the attackers, and judged from the determination with which they were invested that they planned to smother the fire of the defenders and then break open the sodhouse. If the assault succeeded, the annihilation of the nesters would follow as the night the day, but the men inside the dwelling had already sensed this for themselves and were now shooting with a speed and accuracy that was emptying saddles at a rate that must make the price of success unacceptably high if it continued.

Rifle at his shoulder, Wells let the range decrease and then put his Winchester to work, scoring hit after hit; but, regardless of the casualties, the impetus of the charge remained, and the sheer weight of over-spurred horseflesh brought the surviving riders onwards until the wave broke about the sodhouse and the fight was again reduced to cursing individuals and gun against gun.

Horses wheeled past Wells' corner position. Pistols flashed at him. He fired at every target that presented. The air stank of powdersmoke and horsesweat. Moonlight touched faces and steel; the racket echoed into the prairie. Then a fist struck Wells between the eyes. Staggered, he tried to bring his assailant down with a bullet, but his rifle clicked emptily. Reversing the long gun, he swung its butt as a club, bruised the back of the man who had punched him, and probably broke the right leg of the rider who passed him next. But then a horse boring in from the right gave his body a glancing blow and threw him to the ground.

Winded, he lay under the front wall of the sodhouse, expecting to be snuffed out at any instant. Guns blazed down at him, and he felt small thuds as bullets entered the dirt around his frame. Conscious of what he was doing only as if another were doing it, he shucked his sixgun and fired among the shapes that came and went above him. A rider uttered a shout, and for Wells the sound identified the Broken S's segundo, Evan Rank. The little man threatened, trying to steady himself for a shot and, as a matter of necessity — since he had rather liked the under-foreman as a person — Wells blasted a slug into the other's body. The segundo cried out, and folded onto his mount's neck, then swung away, taking a few shocked comrades with him. In that moment it seemed to Wells that everything changed magically, for the crash of the guns along the front wall of the sodhouse subdued all answering explosions and the riders from the Broken S who had still been pressing the fight at the other end of the building appeared to lose their nerve and went drubbing southwards in full retreat. Wells was sure this time that Spearman's people had had enough, and that the battle was over.

Clambering slowly to his feet, Wells dusted himself off as a matter of habit and looked somewhat dazedly down the moonlit countryside. Then he reloaded the fired chambers of his Colt and holstered the weapon. After that he located and picked up his Winchester, feeding several cartridges into the rifle and pumping one into the barrel. Now he began a quick round of the bodies lying near the sodhouse, and found four dead men and six wounded. He could just discern other shapes lying at greater distances from the dwelling, but the appearance of Jake Enderby at his elbow stopped him from going further afield. 'Will they come back?' Enderby asked anxiously.

'Maybe,' Wells said carefully, raising

an eyebrow as he heard a baby's thin wailing from inside the sodhouse. 'But I don't think so.'

'You think we've seen 'em off?'

'Uh, huh. Sounds like your other worry is over too.'

'Yes,' Enderby replied, almost happily. 'The little fellow came in a hurry when he set about it. Maybe he wanted to take a hand.'

'Maybe,' Wells agreed. 'Anybody hurt indoors?'

'Farrell went and scalded his foot when he kicked over some boiling water. He won't die of it.'

'That's all?'

'The whole lot.'

'Lucky,' Wells observed.

'I told you the Lord would provide,' called the listening Martha Enderby from the doorway of the sodhouse.

'He surely did, ma'am,' Wells acknowledged.

Jake Enderby rested a hand on Wells' right shoulder. 'I figured we'd lost you one time.'

148

'I don't die so easy,' Wells said. 'But it was touch-and-go.'

'We made 'em pay,' Enderby enthused.

'The general will never make an all-out attack on you again,' Wells assured him. 'I reckon the Broken S has lost more than half its number, dead or wounded.'

'We owe it to you, Wells,' Enderby admitted. 'If you hadn't come along and talked some backbone into us, we'd have died where we stood.'

'We had our luck, Jake,' Wells said soberly. 'Let's leave it there.'

'Suits me,' Enderby agreed. 'You ain't going to leave us?'

'Not tonight anyhow,' Wells answered, turning his head as a hollow groan from nearby told of a wounded man who was perhaps recovering consciousness. 'I don't know what we're going to do about their wounded.'

'There's no room for them indoors,' Jake Enderby said.

'We've no medical help either.'

'There's a cave behind Beacon Ridge.'

'How big is it, Jake?'

'Hold several men. But it's wet as the Great Lakes.'

'Every damned thing is wet over there,' Wells growled. 'We can only do the best we're able. You'd better call your sons out here.'

'Hold on!' Enderby urged, peering southwards. 'I think I see a rider coming. 'Do you think it's a trap?'

'I doubt it,' Wells said, spotting the horseman for himself and watching the fellow come to a halt about fifty yards away.

'Hello, the house!' the rider shouted.

'Straw?' Wells demanded, recognising the hired killer's voice. 'What is it you want?'

'Our dead and wounded.'

'That's a bit more luck, Jake,' Wells said quietly. 'Want to tell him?'

'You tell him.'

'You can have them — and good riddance,' Wells shouted. 'Come and fetch 'em. Not all of you, mind. Just two men. I leave it up to you who they're to be.'

'Okay,' Straw said resignedly. 'I'll send two men along.' He paused, and seemed about to turn his horse away; but then he checked and asked: 'Wells?'

'You know it is!'

'I see,' Straw responded knowingly. 'You g'damned Benedict Arnold! That all friendship means to you? What's the general going to say?'

'No more than I guess he's already said,' Wells replied. 'I don't give a damn anyway? I hope that tonight will teach him and his wife that they don't have command over life and death. Tell him I said so.'

'You may be sure!' Straw declared, wheeling his mount away this time and riding off southwards.

'This ain't finished for you, Wells,' Enderby said.

'I don't think it is,' Wells admitted, passing his rifle to the older man and then walking away to make a quick catch of four horses that had lost their riders during the fight and had come to a standstill on some grass not far off. Tying the animals' reins together, he left them bunched a short distance to the west of the Enderby home; then he went and caught some more, for he could see no harm in helping the two men whom Straw had said he would send along to that extent. The sooner the dead and wounded had been removed from the area, the sooner would all at Beacon Ridge be able to relax. For his part, Wells was just about cross-eyed with fatigue and could imagine nothing better than a few hours sleep.

The two men from Straw turned up within ten minutes. They were ordinary cowboys and not the least aggressive any longer. Left to them, Wells felt certain that there would have been no fighting in the first place. Nevertheless, he felt obliged to watch them at their work, and ended up helping out — as did Jake Enderby and his sons — but it was still past midnight when the pair from the Broken S were able to lead away the grim train of dead and crippled men that bore witness to Amos Spearman's defeat at the hands of John Wells and the despised nesters.

With the area to themselves again, Wells and his companions walked back to the sodhouse. At this hour, the moon rode high in the empty heavens and the country glistened. After recovering his rifle — and arranging a roster of guards with Madison, Farrell, and the two Enderby sons — Wells declared his intention of sleeping near the not far distant waterhole; and, after 'goodnights' all round, he took himself off in the direction of the ridge, came to his horse again, slipped his Winchester back into its sheath, then unshipped his blanket-roll and laid out his bed close to the spring-hole. After that he stretched out and covered himself, falling asleep almost instantly, and his dreamless slumber took him through the rest of the night and up to six o'clock the next morning, when he was shaken awake by Sam Enderby and informed that it was time for him to take over the look-out from the other Enderby boy on the ridge.

Rising, full of yawns and thick-headed, Wells put his blanket-roll together again and restored it to his cantle. Then he went to the spring-hole and shoved his head neck-deep into the icy water that filled it. After that he clambered up the southern face of Beacon Ridge and relieved Les Enderby of the watch, sitting down on the flat-topped rock which the other had just vacated and gradually forcing the slowness out of his wits as he muttered the twelve-times table over to himself and gazed northwards.

The land stretched vast and pastel-shaded behind the morning mists, and Wells discerned distantly stirring herds, their movements at one with the slow wreathing of the vapour. Before long he found himself wondering what was happening at the Broken S ranch house, but with curiosity rather than fear, for he had the feeling today that this guard duty was superfluous to the real needs of the nesters. The Broken S had been given a drubbing, and it was impossible that either money or threats would ever bring about another ride against the nesters. Amos Spearman would either have to develop a more peaceful method of getting rid of the hoe-men or learn to live with them. If high-stomached, the general was no fool, and Wells was of the opinion that the man would ultimately perceive that the amount of land being lost to the plough was in fact quite small and also realize that even the biggest cattle outfit could only expand so far and remain a sound business.

Wells heard a rumbling from his belly. He thought about breakfast, and pondered whether to go down to his horse and get some grub out of his saddlebags. He was still thus engaged, when a rider emerged from a bank of mist just beyond the swale that ran along the northern foot of Beacon Ridge and came to a halt, peering upwards.

Rising, Wells stepped into a position where he could be seen by the man below, at the same time recognising the other as Jack Straw. It was possible, of course, that Straw was here to talk with the nesters, on his employer's behalf, but Wells was instinctively sure that the hired killer was looking for him. 'If it's me you want, Straw,' he called through cupped hands, 'you've found me.'

'Good,' Straw responded. 'Feared I might have to hang about — or even ride round to the homesteads.' He lifted his Stetson, and sleeved back some hair off his brow, lowering the hat again and snugging it down above his ears. 'Mrs Spearman sent me.'

'What does she want?'

'Your guts.'

'Figures,' Wells conceded, snorting into laughter. 'Would she like me to send her the rope to hang me with?'

'I'm sure she'd be right pleased

with that,' Straw mocked. 'She told me to tell you that we've got Joan Hastings and little Annie with us on the Broken S, and that it might be good for them if you turned up at the house shortly as an earnest for their safety. What do you say to me, Wells?'

Wells stood and stared at the man below. For that moment he was too shocked to say anything at all.

7

Despite his feeling of impotence, Wells forced himself to think calmly. Until now he had accepted Madeleine Spearman as no more than a vindictive woman who was also a bad enemy, but now he found himself starting to realize how deep her hatred went and how perceptive and resourceful she could really be. Yet he could also see that she was gambling here. For while he had betrayed an interest in Mrs Hastings and her small daughter, dark Madeleine must be aware that he had merely helped them in passing and that there was no bond or obligation present.

But if Mrs Spearman's lever had little bite where the strict realities were concerned, it did once again involve the matter of common decency. Madeleine had him weighed up well enough to be reasonably certain that he would not dismiss the plight of Joan Hastings and her child as of no consequence to him. The matter had been directed at him as a duty. Though he found it hard to believe that Mrs Spearman would do actual bodily harm to mother and daughter, he could not be entirely sure about it. He suspected that Madeleine was mentally warped and, because of that, in some degree unpredictable. Therefore, he could bank on nothing where she was concerned.

Yes, common decency had it. He could not leave Joan Hastings and little Annie in Mrs Spearman's clutches. True, delivering up his own person to her — with the terrifying risk to his life which this would entail — might not free the pair, but it ought to take the heat out of the situation for the minute, and that must be some kind of worthy end in itself. Indeed, it appeared the most that he could do for mother and daughter as the matter shaped now. 'All right, Straw,' he called heavily. 'You can tell Mrs Spearman that I will put in an appearance at the ranch house before the morning is over.'

'How if you ride back with me right now, Wells?'

'Did Mrs Spearman ask for that?'

'No,' Straw admitted reluctantly. 'But what's the objection? It might as well be soon as late.'

'Sling your hook, mister!' Wells advised. 'I want my breakfast. A man should always have his breakfast when he's got a busy day ahead of him.'

'I hope that'll satisfy her.'

'That's how it is, Straw.'

'Only — '

'What?'

'She means it, Wells,' the assassin replied gravely. 'She told me she'd cut the gizzard out of the woman and choke the child, if you didn't show up. Take that as honest help.'

'I hear her rattle,' Wells commented.

'They ain't men,' Straw reminded, slowly turning his mount away, though he kept his face twisted towards the ridge. 'They don't think like us.' Now his features turned to the front and he covered a few yards of his return journey before adding: 'Be seeing you!'

Wells did not respond. He was appalled by what he had just heard. When a Satanic character like Straw showed signs of disgust, there was much to be feared. Murder of the most heartless and sadistic kind had been threatened. Madeleine Spearman sounded even more crazy than he had judged, and he must be careful to do nothing that might goad her into killing. Always allowing, of course, that the woman and Jack Straw could have planned to reduce him to the state of mind in which he now found himself. He must not lose sight of any state of cunning that could be involved; which meant that a deeper and more knowing part of his mind could be trying to tell him something of great importance. But what?

After standing against the sky for a minute or two longer, Wells made his way down the back of the ridge and returned to the spot where he had slept. His horse was grazing around the edges of the waterhole, and he went to the animal and unhooked his canteen from the saddle. Uncorking the bottle, he washed it out, then filled it with liquid from the spring and corked up again, restoring the canteen to its place on his pommel. After that, brow furrowed and mind darting back and forth, he took a hunch of bread from his nearside saddlebag and ate it to the last crumb; then, in a moment of decision that nevertheless found him no wiser than he had been at the start, he went to his mount's head and then walked the brute round to the front door of the sodhouse, where he found Jake Enderby sitting on a three-legged stool, with a churchwarden pipe in his left hand and a mug of coffee in his right. 'You going?' Jake inquired, both his expression and tones indicating that he felt disappointed and let down.

'Must,' Wells answered. 'Absolutely no choice.' And he went on to tell

Enderby of his recent conversation with Jack Straw and to explain how he had come to meet Joan Hastings and little Annie the previous day. He left out nothing relevant to the threat against mother and child, and went into detail where he had to, concluding: 'I'm in trouble when Mrs Spearman gets her hands on me, but I can't risk what she might do to mother and child if I don't show up at the ranch house.'

'I can see you've got no choice,' Enderby said — 'bein' the kind of man you are. You seem born to fight other folk's battles. We met them Hastingses on the way down here. Nice people. I'm mighty sorry to hear he's dead.' Jake thumbed at the bowl of his pipe. 'Look, Wells. You done good by us. Can we do anything for you?'

'No, Jake,' Wells replied. 'You people have enough to do to look after yourselves. It's my problem, and I'll do the best I can with it.'

'But it's serious!' Enderby protested. 'You could get killed.'

'The possibility's there,' Wells admitted, climbing onto his horse. 'I've told you how it is, so you know about it. Goodbye.'

'Fare-you-well.'

Wells gigged into motion. He rode a few hundred yards towards the rising sun, then turned round the eastern shoulder of Beacon Ridge and headed north, eyes roving about him all the time, for he feared a sudden swoop by Broken S horsemen that would make a prisoner of him and thus take away the choice he still had of going where he wished.

His mind was again troubled by those subconscious stirrings. Without reducing his vigilance, he let his vague thoughts shape into whatever form they wished and gather strength, and suddenly he was conscious of a very different view of where he ought to be going than had been with him previously. For he now perceived that, whatever her malice towards him, Madeleine Spearman still had her husband to contend with and would hardly have risked a kidnapping of which the general was aware — especially as he, Wells, the man for whom the victims were to be used as bait, could ride around all possible traps and call in the Amarillo law, which might deny jurisdiction in cattle matters but would not dare turn a blind eye to actual criminal activities that were taking place on the Broken S. By this same token it was almost certain that, while the abduction of Joan Hastings and her little daughter could be accepted as a fact, the kidnapped pair were not being held on the Broken S ranch site itself but at some other spot on the spread.

Wells' imagination faltered before the possibilities that his reasoning had opened up. Just how many hiding places would there be on a ranch that was simply vast in extent? Dozens? Scores? Hundreds? More? He suspected the latter, and knew from experience that, when you were dealing with numbers of that magnitude and didn't even know the terrain intimately, the chances of lighting on that one secret place where the kidnapped pair were being held were so remote that a search could amount to the most wearying form of self-punishment.

Yet following up on the mental glimmerings which had brought him to his present state of enlightenment was the vision of a line shack — the one which Jack Straw had spoken of as being to the far west of the ranch site when they had first talked together. True, most of what Straw had said at that time had subsequently proved to be a pack of lies, but Wells nevertheless had the feeling that the line shack mentioned really did exist and had simply been the peg on which Straw had hung the spurious story of his day. Going on the manner in which the human mind worked, Straw, assuming he'd had charge of the abduction — and that really didn't warrant doubt, since he was the only double-dyed villain now at dark Madeleine's command — would most likely have had the kidnapped woman and child taken to a spot which had recently made its mark on his imagination, and the line shack could have been just the place.

The problem of time abruptly troubled Wells. He looked skywards and around, considering the state of the light and reckoning the time to be about eight a.m. If he pushed his horse a little, he should be able to cover several miles in two hours — sufficient distance anyhow to bring him in sight of the building he sought — and if the line shack wasn't there, he should still be able to get back to the Broken S ranch house in time to say that he had kept his word to make a morning call on Mrs Spearman. He didn't like it. The time element was too tight, and there were too many question marks involved. But his plan seemed about as near to covering the best possibilities as he could get.

Wells fetched his mount's head into

the west. Then using his spurs harder than was his wont, he sent the brute galloping away from the low glare of the climbing sun and kept it at full stretch for as long as he dared. He covered five or six miles in this spell, and then allowed the horse to slow by no more than a third, so that they went on eating up ground in the best possible ratio to the mount's output of energy. Altogether, the horse, well-fed and rested, behaved perfectly, and neither trip nor stumble interrupted the even tenor of their journey westwards.

The scene, increasingly wide beyond Beacon Ridge, became ever more so as the miles went by, with the sky lowering its mighty cup of blue to fit the horizon's circle and traceries of high rock floating into bodiless peaks beyond the misty edges of the union. But beauty and boredom were present in equal measures, and Wells might have dozed in his saddle had the anxieties of his mission not kept his blood flowing quickly throughout. He saw herds of cows often and feared being seen by herders, but in fact he saw no ranchmen around and could only ascribe this to the shortage of labour which the Broken S must be suffering after last night's battle with the nesters.

There came a moment when Wells felt that he had ridden far enough west. He must be nearing the limits of the Spearman grass by now, and he believed it time to make the final attempt to discover whether or not the line shack spoken of by Jack Straw really did exist. Spotting a conical mound at no great distance ahead, he decided to climb it, stipulating that, if he could see nothing of the shack from up there, he would accept that the shack had no existence, face about, and then ride due east towards the Broken S ranch site. He went on for five minutes more, then climbed the little hill and, only too aware of how exposed he was upon its summit, drew rein and gazed slowly from left to right, glimpsing what could only be the building he sought standing in the bay formed by an irregular half-circle of stone-heaps and thorn trees about a mile to the northwest of him.

Moving to his right, Wells slanted off the hillock. He began closing on the shack. Though he had so far seen nothing to make him believe that the building was occupied, he started using the land to conceal something of his presence. There was a system of shallow landfolds in this neighbourhood, and by careful use of these tucks he was able to stay below the level of the shack during most of his approach. Indeed, when he left the folds he found himself riding wide of the shanty's blind northern end and ideally placed to do what he intended next, which was to skirt round to the rear of the piled rocks and matted thorn trees and work in towards the structure from that direction.

In the event he was partially thwarted in his plan. The thorn trees at the direct rear of the shack were too tightly knitted to let him through, and he was forced to withdraw a short distance to his left and pass into the barrier arc down an irregular channel in the rock and spiky foliage that brought him to a rock-pile about ten yards back from the building's northern end. Dismounting, Wells ground-tied his horse behind the heap of stone and then, doubled low, moved into the clear and advanced cautiously on the shack. Then, all at once, he was glad of his care, for a slight movement on his right, followed by a snuffling noise, caused him to turn his head sharply to his right and see, near the shack's southern end, two horses that were tethered to pegs at the middle of a small square of thick grass. A third mount, he also perceived in this moment, had been tied to the chimney-pipe which curved out of the building's rear wall and then pointed skywards. Obviously then, for all its apparent stillness, the shanty was occupied and, though he did not believe it the case, he could have been seen approaching by eyes watching from within.

Drawing his revolver, Wells began hurrying his movements a trifle. He dived into the shelter of the wall at the shack's northern end and then trod stealthily to the corner ahead. Rounding the angle, he crept now along the erection's front wall and came to a window that was located between the corner that he had just left and the shack's entrance. Pressing his back close to the log-built wall behind him, Wells slid a glance through the window's dusty glass and saw sleeping figures inside. Two big men — Sam Colley and Ben Rearden — were seated on benches at the middle of the floor and slumped over the table before them. Their foreheads rested on their arms, and Wells could hear the broad-backed pair snoring rhythmically. Beside the wall at the building's further end stood a bunk, and upon the bunk lay Joan Hastings. She was sleeping a sleep of exhaustion similar to the men's, and her daughter, little Annie, lay in the crook of her right arm, also deeply oblivious to the world and its troubles for now. Feeling a certain satisfaction, Wells nodded to himself and reflected that his bump of events had not let him down. Now all he had to do was take full advantage of a situation which had placed the guards on the woman and child virtually at his mercy.

Stepping past the window, Wells came to the shack's door and stopped before it, lifting his left hand to the latch. Then he gently depressed the thumb-rest and the cross-bar lifted, allowing him to push the door inwards on what seemed like silent hinges, but quite suddenly the metal squeaked shrilly and the previous hush was lost in the startled gasp of a man coming quickly awake and lifting his head from the table to peer dazedly across at the door, a curse escaping his thick lips as he went for his revolver.

The features into which Wells gazed were those of Ben Rearden and, taking swift advantage of the fact that he was fully awake and the other wasn't, he crossed the yard or so of floor between him and the table in a single stride and clipped the big man across the crown with his gun barrel. Rearden slumped forward again, waking Sam Colley in the process, but Colley had his back to Wells and had little idea of what was happening as he, too, sank back into a sleeping posture when the barrel of the rescuer's gun made another thudding pass above the table.

There was a stirring from the bunk on the left, then a child's whimper and, looking that way, Wells saw Joan Hastings raised on her left elbow and gazing at him with startled eyes, the frightened child now clinging tightly to her neck. 'Mr — Wells,' the woman murmured thickly.

'Him and no other,' Wells agreed. 'I've come to get you out of this.'

'What on earth *is* happening?' the blonde demanded, still bewildered and sounding faintly querulous. 'Those awful men descended on our cabin during the early hours and made prisoners of Annie and me. They put us on a horse, then brought us here across the plain. Why?'

'Rearden and Colley didn't tell you?'

'They told me nothing.'

'It's possible they don't fully know themselves,' Wells said thoughtfully. 'It comes to this, ma'am. Phil Baker, the foreman of the Broken S and the man who shot your husband, drew on me, and I was forced to kill him. He was Madeleine Spearman's lover, and she now wants me dead in revenge for his death. She knew I'd given you some help — and that I was maybe a bit interested in what happened to you and Annie — so she had you and the child seized and then used you both as bait for the trap that she set for me. Luckily, I saw through her game and came here on a hunch. Thank God you and Annie haven't been harmed. I aim to keep it that way. Are you ready to travel, ma'am?'

'Yes,' the woman answered, her eyes

wide as her imagination appeared to fill in the gaps in what he had told her. 'Where to?'

'I reckon it will have to be Beacon Ridge for now,' Wells replied. 'I hope I can fix you up with the Madisons until I can get things sorted out.'

'What do you mean by that, Mr Wells?'

'I only wish I knew,' he responded.

'Sir, you are not responsible for Annie and me,' Mrs Hastings said flatly, clearly uncertain as to whether or not she was actually offended by his solicitousness. 'We can look after ourselves.'

'Joan,' Wells advised bluntly, 'don't talk like a fool. I've just tried to tell you why I'm doing this. You might say I got you into it, and now it's up to me to get you out. If you figure I'm out to take advantage somehow, you're plumb loco. I know you're a widow new-made, and that you loved your husband dearly. But you and Annie can't help yourselves. You're lost in

176

this wilderness of grass, and you know it in your heart. I was brought up in this land, and I do know it. When all's done, ma'am, and I've resolved this trouble — likely with the help of the law yonder at Amarillo — you will be entirely free to make whatever arrangements you wish for Annie and yourself. Until then, as a matter of pure common sense, I suggest you let me do what's best for you both.'

'Tell me,' the blonde challenged. 'If I said that I meant to walk out of that door with Annie, right now, and intended to do exactly as I pleased thereafter, would you try to stop me?'

Wells did not hesitate; because he knew he must not. 'No, ma'am.'

She studied him for a moment, and he met her gaze with steady eyes. 'Very well,' she said finally. 'I will be pleased — and grateful — to put Annie and myself in your hands.'

'Fine,' he said, gesturing for her to get off the bunk. 'We've wasted enough time over that.'

'I'm sorry,' she said, swinging her booted feet to the floor and standing up with Annie in her arms.

'Don't be,' Wells returned, trying to keep the pity out of his gaze as he looked on her forlorn and dishevelled person. 'You have your own integrity, ma'am, and it's for you to know what that is.'

She nodded comprehendingly. 'Is there a horse?'

'I think it must be the one tied to the chimney-pipe at the back of the shack,' Wells answered, signalling for her to precede him out of the door.

The woman stepped into the open, still carrying her daughter, and she turned to the left, obviously with the intention of following the walls round to the building's rear. Holstering his Colt, Wells walked after her, and the three of them soon came to the horse tethered at the back of the shanty. Joan Hastings set Annie down; then, as the woman was preparing to mount and Wells to free the animal, a light footfall sounded at the corner of the shanty behind them and a voice that Wells recognised as Jack Straw's commanded: 'Freeze, folks! You've gone as far as you're going. In fact I reckon you've gone as far as you're ever going!'

Wells feared they could have heard the truth. Straw had them completely in his power. Clearly, they had talked too long and watched too little.

8

Wells felt Straw take his pistol. Then he glanced at Mrs Hastings. He saw upon her face a look of such hopelessness and disappointment that he turned sick inside. There was, too, a kind of awful acceptance about her demeanour as she picked up her child again and held Annie tightly to her breast, and this made him feel like an inadequate and posturing bungler.

He had been too sure of himself, and taking too much for granted. He had made two bad mistakes. The first one had been in underestimating Straw's intelligence, and the second had been in placing trust in what the hired killer had said about riding back to Madeleine Spearman and reporting that he, Wells, would be arriving at the Broken S during the morning. He could also be said to have committed a third serious error in imagining that because he had correctly followed his enemy's mind he had eliminated the possibility of further trickery. While he didn't believe that Straw and Mrs Spearman had actually planned that things should turn out as they had, he now realized that he should have kept a closer watch on his back trail and remembered that others too went on thinking and anticipating.

'Back into the shack,' Straw ordered. 'Walk straight ahead, then round the other end of the building.'

Joan Hastings again went first. Once more Wells moved after her. Straw's threatening presence closed at his heels. He felt the muzzle of the assassin's pistol give him a prod at every second or third step. There was nothing for it but to obey. It would have been an act of suicide to attempt rounding on a gun so near.

Soon Mrs Hastings re-entered the shack, and Straw said:'Sit on the bunk, lady. You stand near her, Wells.'

Wells stepped inside behind the woman. He waited for her to sit down, then took up a stance near the head of the bunk. After that Straw moved indoors and closed up behind him; then, his Colt covering the small area which contained the prisoners, he backed off a little and examined the two men who were still slumped senseless at the table. 'These boys have got nasty bumps on their heads,' he remarked. 'They're going to wake up mad as hell. I figure they'll be wanting to get their own back.'

'I suppose you'll be sending one of that pair to fetch Madeleine Spearman,' Wells said tightly.

Straw smirked at him, faintly questioning.

'She's running the show, isn't she?'

'You bet she is, mister,' Straw agreed. 'Why bother to ask? When you get right down to it, Amos is no more than a figurehead. As for Mrs Spearman, she'll be here long before you thought. I never did think you'd ride into the ranch yard like a good boy; so I wasn't alone when I rode out to Beacon Ridge first thing this morning. I had another man with me, and I left him hidden at a spot nice and handy to watch any move you might make into the country, while I kept an eye on the route to the ranch. You proved a mite smart, though, and suddenly turned left after leavin' Beacon Ridge. I wondered what in hell you were up to for a moment, but I soon twigged your game, and I sent the other guy back to the house to report where I reckoned you were headed. I expect Madeleine Spearman to get here within the hour.'

'Congratulations, Straw,' Wells said ironically.

'On what?' Straw asked narrowly. 'It was a mistake to speak of this shack.'

'On your luck,' Wells mocked. 'One day you'll get so smart you will out-smart yourself. You see if you don't.'

'You talk about luck,' Straw rasped. 'You don't know how lucky you are, Wells. If it wasn't that Mrs Spearman is saving you for herself, you'd have been dead hours ago. You made an easy shot at least six times coming here, and a perfect one when you were perched on top o'that hill.'

'I can see how that would be,' Wells admitted. 'You're confessing your trade, you cheap murderer!'

Straw gave a chuckle that was low and ugly. 'Cheap I am not, Mr Wells, and tomorrow is still mine. Can you say that?'

'Are you sure that the lady of the Broken S won't let you down at the last,' Wells asked cynically. 'The young wives of old husbands get indulged, but they often have shallow purses.'

'When you've got as much on somebody as I've got on Madeleine Spearman,' Straw said with an equal cynicism, 'they can't help but be generous.'

'Watch your back,' Wells cautioned.

'*I* always do,' the hired killer stressed.

At the table, Sam Colley uttered a groan. Then, a deep breath roaring in his huge chest, he stirred back to consciousness and held his hairy face between his thick, stubby-fingered hands.

'Nice mornin', old partner,' Straw greeted unfeelingly. 'Been sleeping in?'

'May the devil take you, Straw!' Colley snarled, lurching erect and shifting his fingers to the sides of his skull. 'My head!'

'You must expect to hurt a little when some varmint's bent a gun barrel over your crown,' Straw said, still mocking as he indicated Wells. 'There's the guy who did it to you.'

Colley blinked red-eyed at Wells. He stood like a gorilla, bent slightly and with hands hanging beside his knees. Then he swung a left, but Wells rocked backwards and the blow missed his chin. Colley plainly had thoughts of repeating the punch, but then his expression told that the effort had cost him more pain than it had brought relief and, baring his teeth in utter hatred, he turned away from the table and staggered to the door, wrenching his way into the open air.

'Where d'you think you're going?' Straw called after him.

'Need some air,' came the answer. 'And a drink from the well. My mouth tastes like a — '

'Lady present,' Wells interrupted. 'Two in fact.'

'Your pardon, ma'am,' Colley shouted back, an unexpected note of genuine contrition in his voice.

'Don't be long!' Straw warned. 'You and Ben Rearden are supposed to be the guards here — not me.'

'Aw, fry!' Colley responded from somewhere beyond the southern end of the shack.

There was silence in the building. Wells folded his arms and looked down at the toes of his boots. Several minutes went by. Then Rearden made a less obvious return to his senses than Colley had done, suddenly raising his head and just sitting there, no sound on his lips.

'Sam's gone to the well,' Straw abruptly advised. 'You do likewise, Ben — and tell that sack o' pig-meat to get his butt back in here!'

'All right,' Rearden sniffed, glancing at Wells uncertainly.

'Yeah, he clubbed you,' Straw said in a profoundly bored voice. 'You won't die of it.'

Scowling to himself, Rearden walked shakily out of the shack and went in the direction that Colley had gone before him. Another twelve or fifteen minutes passed, during which Colley showed no sign of himself and Rearden also remained absent, and Straw spent much of the time muttering to himself and fidgeting, though never for an instant did he lose his concentration where watching the captives were concerned.

Rearden and Colley returned together. They had obviously been bathing their heads and taking a rest. Their expressions warned that they were in no mood to suffer further criticism, and their eyes dared Straw to start anything of the kind. The hired killer opened his mouth on threatened sourness, but hesitated, then forced a grin and asked: 'You guys feeling better?'

'We'll do,' Colley said for them both. 'Mrs Spearman and a few of the hands are comin' in. We just saw 'em'.

'How far?' Straw asked.

'Mebbe a mile,' Colley replied. 'She's floggin' that black of hers.'

'Surprises me,' Rearden commented. 'When I last saw that woman — afore we seized yon lady and her kid — Madeleine had got Phil Baker laid out, pretty as you please in his Sunday best, and was lookin' at him as if she meant never to stop.'

'Sure was hard hit,' Colley agreed.

'God help you, Wells!' Straw exclaimed, smiling cruelly. 'You'll wish my rifle had claimed you yet!'

'You animal!' Joan Hastings flared at the man, coming to sudden life and showing a power of anger which the shocked Wells would never have believed could spring into existence behind her serene loveliness.

'Well, now,' Straw observed wolfishly. 'Maybe you ain't such a lady after all. If you want to have a cuss in front of her, Colley, you have one. She's nothing!'

'Straw, I'm going to feed you your teeth for that one!' Wells promised.

'Not if I feed you six ounces of lead first!' Straw retaliated, lunging at Wells with his Colt and checking the pistol's muzzle only inches from the captive's mouth.

Wells did not flinch. His gaze locked Straw's. He had never been more angry in his life, and the force of his rage lanced from him in his stare. It was Jack Straw who yielded. Gesturing for Colley and Rearden to cover the prisoners now, the hired killer turned away and looked out of the window. 'Here they come,' he said. 'I'll never know what she needs four guys with her for. Be a madness to let them see any part of what's going to happen here.'

Straw retreated from the windowpanes.

He waited a minute, then walked to the door and went outside. Shortly after that the drubbing of hooves became audible in the shack, and the sound increased in volume until the shadows of the approaching mounts and their riders touched the window and showed on the threshold.

Ears straining, Wells heard a few words pass between Straw and Mrs Spearman. They were spoken in the lowest of tones. Then the woman entered the shack. An elegant figure in her black velvet riding habit and veiled top hat of the same colour, she halted before Wells. Her face pallid behind the veil, she considered him for a long moment, tapping the palm of her left hand with a silver-mounted quirt which she held in her right. Then, with a small cry, she drew back the quirt and struck him across the face with such force that his head was driven back against the wall behind him and the whole building shook. Dazed, and bleeding from his right cheek, Wells feared that the one blow would prove an introduction to many, but Madeleine Spearman regained control of herself instantly and stepped back to take what appeared to be a brief but vengeful pleasure in the pain that she had inflicted. Then she glanced across her left shoulder to where Straw stood just inside the door and said: 'I'm pleased with you, Jack. You have served me well.'

'Thank you, ma'am.'

'Now,' the woman said. 'Whatever we do here has to be final, has it not?'

'For keeps,' Straw agreed. 'No other course — if you want to live your best years as a free woman. Your crimes are already bad enough to draw life imprisonment. A judge would speak of kidnapping and criminal conspiracy. If you let Mrs Hastings live, she'll peach for sure; and if you let the child live, how will you explain her?'

'I've thought of all of it, Jack,' Madeleine Spearman said. 'We're a long way down the road to hell.'

'There's no return, ma'am.'

'Then we must be strong,' the dark woman said with finality. 'I want John Wells hanged from a bough in the old fashioned manner. Let him slowly strangle. You can knife Joan Hastings; she's a poor thing. The child can drown in the well. Let it be a grave for the three of them. You can fill it in when all is done.'

'Are you human, Mrs Spearman?' Wells asked in horror. 'There isn't a man here could drown that morsel!'

'Straw!' the woman snapped, gesturing imperiously.

'No, lady,' Straw said, slowly shaking his head. 'Not that. I'll hoist the man for you — and fix it so that he takes a long time to die. I'll even do the woman in; but I'll not murder the child.'

'And you call yourself a man?' Madeleine Spearman asked contemptuously.

'He's man enough,' Wells said

desperately, 'and he's black with sin. But there's a wickedness even hell can't stomach, and that's the killing of a child. Many a swine's been saved from the burning — because he knew where to stop — but there's no redemption for the man who slays an innocent babe. Even Jack Straw knows that!'

'Is it so, Jack?' Mrs Spearman inquired.

Straw hung his head and made no reply.

The dark woman challenged Sam Colley with her eye.

'No, ma'am,' the bearded man said sullenly.

'What about you, Rearden?'

'Not a chance, ma'am,' Rearden retorted, gazing at the child who, finger in mouth, was cowering against her mother, not fully understanding the reason for her fear but clearly feeling it deeply enough for all that. 'Rather would I throw myself into that well.'

'Men!' the dark woman scoffed. 'What cowardly creatures you are at heart! If you're afraid to do it, I'll do it myself.' And, turning towards little Annie, she reached out to snatch her from her mother.

Joan Hastings reacted with the speed of an enraged tigress. Pushing the child aside, she rose from the bunk and threw herself at Madeleine Spearman. Knocking away the dark woman's veiled hat, she seized handfuls of the raven hair that spilled out of Mrs Spearman's silver combs, pulling for all she was worth. Then the weight of the attack toppled both women, and they struck an edge of the table which stood at the centre of the floor. The piece of furniture lifted under the impact and went sliding against the wall at the shack's further end. After that the two women hit the floor in a kick-up of hems and began to fight with all the clawing, biting savagery of the feline kind.

The men were momentarily paralysed by the suddenness and ferocity of it all; but Wells — who had never stopped looking for the chance to make something out of what had previously looked like an impossible situation — recovered that much faster than the rest because he must and, glimpsing a clear line to the window, propelled himself away from the spot where he stood beside the head of the bunk and dived headlong at the glass, covering his face with crossed arms and shutting his eyes. Next instant his arrowing weight met the window and tore its frame and panes out of their flimsy settings, and bits and pieces went showering to the ground ahead of him as his body passed through the aperture and came to rest outside.

Conscious that everything had to be done before the shocked men, both inside the shack and out, could recover their wits and act to thwart him, he forced himself to his feet and settled in a trice that he was going to his left. Then, doubled low, he raced along the shack's front wall and rounded the corner at its northern end, speeding westwards after that as he made for the thorn trees and rock-piles at the back of the place.

Voices started shouting behind him. He heard Jack Straw's tones issue the command to kill him anyhow at all. Then he sensed rapid movements at the front of the shack. Feet pursued; pistols began to bang; slugs whizzed by him; a ricochet shrilled and a severed twig jumped off a nearby thorn branch and fell at his feet. He ran faster still. A bullet burned through the slack of his right trouser-leg. Panic threatened; the pulses hammered in his throat. His feet were fairly flying now, yet he sought to go quicker still — and it seemed absurd that he couldn't — but good sense shrieked at him that if he did gain that extra yard, he would only lose his rhythm and his balance also.

Stone which was stained and cracked rushed at him, and he perceived rainbow colours where a spider's web stretched between thorns. Then he achieved cover, and saw his horse standing on the left. Turning in beside the animal, he reached for the jutting stock of his Winchester, but in the same moment he heard Straw yell: 'Don't just sit on them horses, you dummies! Get round the back of those trees! Cut him off!'

Wells stopped reaching for his rifle. There were seven men back at the shack — enough to loosely ring the area, if he gave them the chance; but, if he acted now and left the thorn trees and stone-heaps by the route that he had entered them, he ought to be able to beat the encircling movement and gain sufficient room to make a getaway westwards.

He freed his horse, and swung onto its back. Then he sent the creature nosing north of west. Sensing his need, it threaded the numerous obstructions before him without any guidance and soon burst into the clear. Yanking left, Wells glanced right. He saw a horseman appear not fifty yards away. The rider sent up a shout that must have been heard in Amarillo, then began emptying a sixgun in the fugitive's direction.

Ducking under the lead, Wells drove his spurs into his mount's flanks. The horse lunged for the prairie, hooves kicking divots, and seconds later they came to the familiar view of undulating grasses, with buffalo visible at one spot and a small herd of buck scudding at another. Wells had no plan. The space was there and he galloped his horse down the middle of it. Two or three guns were now cracking and blasting in his wake, but the noise seemed to be receding. He felt sure that he was going to escape, and the belief stirred his mind to frenzied activity. He couldn't just bolt for it; such an action would negate all that had gone before. He had Joan Hastings and Annie to think about; mother and child were in dire peril. He must do something for them. But what? The numbers back there were too many for him. If he went at it recklessly and got himself killed, that would be the end of the woman and her daughter too. He must stay alive, even if that meant temporarily abandoning the pair, for he didn't think that Madeleine Spearman would risk murdering them with him still on the loose.

Then came an example of Man proposes. There had been silence at Wells' back for several moments; but now a single shot rang out. In the same split second, he felt a violent contraction of his mount's inside, and then the brute sighed to itself and went down flat on its belly, legs outflung, the abruptness of its fall bouncing Wells out of the saddle and starting him into a series of somersaults that ended a full dozen yards beyond the animal where he came to rest upon his back with the sky swooping at him and unconsciousness threatening as the light came and went.

Only the knowledge that he must not give in to the dark kept him aware. Making a supreme effort, which was largely powered by fear, he scrambled to his feet and looked back over the range which he had recently covered, seeing four men who were sitting their horses against the arc of thorn trees behind the shack and aiming rifles at him now. He saw the weapons puff smoke, and heard their detonations bark. Only one bullet passed close enough to scare him, but he was reminded that he must get the Winchester off his downed horse before the riders yonder began to advance on him and their shooting became an even worse threat to his life than it had already proved.

Rising, Wells legged it unsteadily back to where his mount lay. One glance was enough to tell him that the stallion was dead. A bullet had entered its rectum and driven on through into its vitals. He was saddened by the creature's death, but his sorrow had to remain vaguely felt for the present, since there was so much here that mattered more; and he threw himself down behind the carcass and drew his Winchester out of its saddleholster, cocking it with a snap of his right wrist.

Resting the barrel of the rifle on the dead mount's side, he watched his enemies start towards him and lined his sights on the man that drew into the lead. He fired a miss, too shaky yet to lay a clean gun. Pumping the ejector, he tried again, with the same result, and after a third miss his hammer snapped into an empty barrel. Swearing in his frustration, he went to his belt after more ammunition, and began forcing shells into the Winchester's magazine as he saw the figures of Colley and Rearden come riding into view around the northern edge of the rock and vegetation that sheltered the site on which the line shack had been built. It was getting rapidly worse. He would soon have six guns shooting at him.

He was all fingers and thumbs as panic threatened, but he willed himself to be calm and had thrust five cartridges into his Winchester by the time that he realized that he had let the foremost riders from the Broken S get too close and must now drive them back before they got any nearer.

Cocking his rifle once more, he drew a steady bead on the most adventurous of the men across the grass — who was now less than fifty yards away — and squeezed the trigger. The rider opposite instantly dropped his rifle and clapped a hand to his left shoulder, the weight of his reeling torso turning his mount in the same direction and causing it to bear him out of the fight. The hit was sufficient to reduce the ambition of the attackers to close his position from the one side only — since Wells was lying in good cover and they had none — and they broke up and began a shouted discussion, which ended in their fanning into a movement which was obviously intended to put a ring about him. While studying the manoeuvres with a calculating eye, Wells took his chance to thumb a few more bullets into his Winchester and gather his courage; for, as he lacked eyes in the back of his head and two pairs of hands — not to mention a second gun — it looked fairly sure that he would soon be killed from behind. He could only attempt to go out making a brave show of it and trying to take as many of the men from the Broken S with him as he could.

Then, as he believed himself keyed up to fight his last battle, he became aware of a renewed shouting among his enemies and of a pause in their movements as they looked southeastwards. Lifting his head, he peered in the same direction, picking up the flash of guns out there and hearing the shots. Then the Broken S riders showed abrupt signs of agitation and seemed to lose all interest in him. They started leaving the field, spurring for full gallop, and looked to be heading back towards the shack.

No longer threatened, Wells stood up and gazed across the grass. His eyes focused now upon the four charging riders whom he had clearly to thank for his survival. He recognised the unmistakable angularity of the Enderbys, Jake and Les, and thought the third man could be the wide-built Charlie Madison — which meant that Beacon Ridge was well represented in his rescue — but he could not even hazard a guess at the identity of the fourth man. Indeed, he was as sure as made no difference that the fellow was a stranger to him.

Relaxing, Wells let the barrel of his rifle point down the side of his right leg. There still seemed a hint of the miraculous about his deliverance; but he guessed it would all be explained when the four incoming horsemen reached him.

9

A minute or so went by. The riders drew nearer at a rapid pace. Then they reached the point at which Wells could see that he had correctly identified the Enderbys, father and elder son, and Madison too, but that the fourth man was indeed a stranger to him.

He eyed this individual, as the four horsemen reined in a few yards from him. The man was among the biggest that he had ever seen, and had a broad, clean-shaven face, with grave, deep-set eyes, a straight nose, and a mouth that went with a jaw that was full of strength. Wells was certain from the first that the other was a lawman, and this was confirmed for him as he caught a glimpse of the Federal law shield pinned to the black shirt under the fellow's leather waistcoat. 'I thank you, gentlemen from Beacon Ridge,'

Wells said, 'and give you good day, Marshal.'

'John Wells?' the lawman asked formally.

'Sir.'

'I'm Deputy U.S. Marshal Cuthbert Aldridge,' the big man said by way of self-introduction. 'Out of the Fort Worth office. You're not unknown to my boss. How did a man of your calibre get involved in these range troubles?'

'To tell you the truth,' Wells confessed, 'I'm starting to wonder myself. I must have been crazy to ever think of throwing in with Amos Spearman.'

'Plumb crazy,' Aldridge agreed. 'I've been talking to Mr Enderby, and it seems you're on the right side now. I don't pretend to understand it, Wells, but in a life of forty-two years I've seen it time and again. When a certain situation needs a certain kind of man, that man always appears. They needed a topnotch lawman in this seedy neck-of-the-woods, and they got one. You seem to have been doing a quite respectable job for those in need.'

'I wish I thought so,' Wells said heavily. 'I seem to have botched things here. I got out from under not long ago, leaving a woman and child in a mighty dangerous situation.'

'I've had those experiences too,' Aldridge said sympathetically. 'No doubt you did the best you could with the cards you were dealt. You can't give more than your life, Wells, and I received the impression you were mighty close to giving it when we hove in sight.'

'No consolation,' Wells said grimly, gazing in the direction of the arc of thorn trees and rock-heaps to the east of him. 'There's a shack yonder, Marshal, and I'm frightened to think what may have happened there in recent minutes. As you may know, I've earned the hatred of a woman who is, I believe, both mad and bad.'

He went on to relate what had taken place in the line shack just prior to his escape, ending: 'If Joan Hastings got herself killed for tackling Madeleine Spearman, and the general's wife has thrown little Annie down the well, you can take me in, Marshal.'

'I'll be taking that woman in,' Aldridge said sternly. 'She's obviously not fit to be around decent folk. Buck up, Wells! There's work for me here, and I want your help.'

'You've got it,' Wells assured him. 'But are we enough, sir. I have the feeling you mean to tackle the Broken S head on, and that is a considerable proposition.'

Aldridge touched the badge on his chest. 'This is *the* law, Wells. Where this shield goes, the full power of the United States Department of Justice goes with it. General Spearman was a fine soldier, and is well-remembered everywhere; but he's no more above the law than you or I. The attention of the United States Marshal for the

Southwest has been called to the manner in which he has treated the settlers in these parts. Spearman is outside the law, and he'd better get back inside it pretty damned quick or he'll find himself in the chaingang with men not fit to lace his boots. Do you understand?'

'Perfectly,' Wells said.

'We're in the right,' Aldridge added. 'We don't have to be afraid of anything or anybody.'

'Marshal,' Jake Enderby said bluntly, 'that's big talk, but your shield's a mighty small one for five of us to hide behind.'

'There's a principle involved, Jake,' Wells explained, hiding a frown, for he feared that Cuthbert Aldridge was a man who saw everything as black or white and could prove a mite too much the fire-eating idealist.

'Have faith in the right,' Aldridge advised, a little indignantly. 'Let's go and have a look at that shack.'

'Being very careful about it,' Wells

cautioned. 'You carry on, Marshal. My horse is dead, and I'm afoot. I'll approach the place through those thorn trees.'

'Very good,' Aldridge agreed, turning his mount's head to the right and signalling for the Beacon Ridge men to follow him as he spurred back into motion.

Carrying his rifle at the trail, Wells broke into a run and headed eastwards behind the horses. He had a quarter of a mile to cover, and did it without slackening pace. Then, shortly after the riders had turned to the left to round the barrier thicket at the shack's rear, Wells entered the thorn trees and carefully threaded a path through the spiked branches until he emerged near the rock-pile behind which he had originally hidden his horse. After that it was only a matter of walking into the space that gave access to the shanty and the land beyond — noting that the mount which he had previously seen tied to the chimney pipe at the back of the structure was still there — and then moving to the front corner of the building's northern end and looking out and around.

He saw at once that there were no horses left on the shack's foreground, and that drained most of his remaining tension, since he was pretty sure that the absence of mounts meant that Madeleine Spearman and those of her employees most to be feared had already withdrawn from the area. Nevertheless, cautious still, he advanced his rifle and catfooted along the shack's front wall until he reached the shattered window. Pausing, he looked through the space and was somewhat surprised to see that there were two people inside. The first, lying motionless at the middle of the floor, was Joan Hastings, and the second, gathered on the bunk in the kind of agony that made further movement almost impossible, was the man whom Wells had wounded in the left shoulder during the recent fight on the grass to the west of them.

Wells made for the door, then entered the shack. He was apprehensive as to the woman's condition but feared still more for her child, of whom there was no trace. For safety's sake, however, he went first to the wounded man and transferred the fellow's Colt to his own holster; then, daring the cowboy to do no more than suffer, he walked to where Joan Hastings lay and knelt beside her. He felt for the arteries in her throat, and strong pulses met his touch. Then he made a quick examination of the blonde's person, but found not race of a serious injury — though there was a bump on her head — and he arrived at the conclusion that she was no worse than unconscious from being struck across the crown with a gun barrel. She'd recover before long.

But there remained the problem of little Annie. What had happened to the child? He must find out, and swiftly. Rising, he swung ferociously on the wounded man and snarled: 'There was a little girl here — little fair-haired mite. What's become of her, boy? If you know, you'd better say fast, because I'm in a bad mood; and when my mood's this bad, I'm not quite responsible!'

'Ease off, mister — ease off!' the wounded man pleaded, putting a large and blood-reddened palm between Wells and himself. 'The child ain't been harmed. Maddie Spearman's got her. I saw her lift the kid onto her saddle just before she rode away from the shack with Straw and some others.'

'How long ago was that?' Wells demanded, feeling some relief.

'Quarter of an hour. Could be a bit less.'

'Why didn't you go with them?'

'I fell off my hoss,' the other explained. 'The old varmint skittered off, and I couldn't catch him to get back on. I sorta stumbled here after that, and saw that lot leavin' as I came round the trees.'

Wells gave his chin a jerk. 'What's your name?'

'Fred Buck.'

'Let's have a look at that shoulder, Buck.'

'My collarbone's smashed,' Buck warned. 'I finished the job when I fell off my hoss. You can't help me. Only a doctor can fix it.'

A shadow fell across the doorway. Cuthbert Aldridge entered. There was barely headroom for his six-feet six-inch frame. Glancing down at Joan Hastings, the deputy U.S. marshal asked: 'Have you looked at her?'

'She's had a tap on the head,' Wells replied. 'I reckon she got it when somebody put a stop to the fight between Madeleine Spearman and her.'

'I'll fetch my canteen,' Aldridge said. 'We'll try and bring her round. What's happened to the child you spoke of?'

Wells told Aldridge what he had himself been told by Buck, including the information that all the Broken S people had pulled out not so long ago.

Nodding, the lawman stepped back

outside, and he reappeared within half a minute with a waterbottle in his hands. Then, squatting beside Mrs Hastings, he uncorked the canteen and sent water splashing into her face. The blonde stirred, and attempted to sit up, but the effort proved too much for her and, groaning, she flattened again. 'What happened?' she muttered thickly. 'Where am I?' Then she seemed to recall everything that had happened to her in a single moment, and she literally fought herself into a sitting position, hands at her temples, and breathed: 'Annie. Where's Annie?' She considered Aldridge almost aggressively. 'Who are you, sir?'

'It's okay, Joan,' Wells said, stepping into the woman's field of vision. 'This is Deputy United States Marshal Cuthbert Aldridge. He's come to straighten Amos Spearman out. Spearman's wife has got Annie. The child's all right.'

'As far as you know?' the blonde inquired accusingly.

'She's all right,' Wells repeated.

'Madeleine Spearman is in company. She can't harm your child while she's on horseback and has men all around her.'

'You're not to worry, ma'am,' Aldridge informed her authoritatively. 'We're going after that bad woman very shortly, and we'll recover your daughter.'

'I'm coming with you,' Mrs Hastings said.

'It would be better if you didn't,' Aldridge told her.

'I'm coming with you, Marshal!'

'For Pete's sake, Aldridge!' Wells exclaimed. 'How do you stop her?' Then he put his hands under the woman's armpits and helped her to her feet. 'There's a horse still standing at the back of this place. I reckon it will bear you and me as far as the Broken S ranch house.'

'We can manage better than that,' Aldridge said. 'Mr Enderby caught a loose horse just south of here, as we rode up.'

'Mine, I reckon,' Fred Buck said from the bunk.

'I'm going to use him,' Wells said.

'Like my gun,' Buck reminded.

'Like your gun,' Wells agreed.

'What about me?' the injured Buck inquired.

'You'll have to endure a while,' Wells said. 'I don't know what will happen at the ranch house when we get there. Or before we get there, if it comes to that. There could be another fight, and more blood flying. But I'll do my best to see that a buckboard is sent out here to pick you up. More I can't promise.'

'It'll have to do,' Buck sighed. 'Hell! I thought a bit o' shooting would be fun!'

'Anything you want off your horse?' Wells asked, shaking his head at the difference between fact and imagination.

'Not a thing,' Buck answered — ' 'cos there ain't a thing there.'

'Here,' Cuthbert Aldridge said, his voice carrying a note of unexpected kindness as he tossed the 'makings' and a bundle of matches onto the bunk at the wounded man's said. 'Don't do it again, sonny.'

'I won't,' Buck said. 'Thankee, Marshal.'

Wells put an arm about Mrs Hastings and helped her out of the door. But, once in the open, she shook off his assistance and headed for the rear of the shack under her own steam. Wells and Aldridge followed her. The three of them came to the chimney pipe at which stood the horse mentioned by Wells. The two men put the blonde on the animal and gave the reins into her hands. Then they walked on either side of the animal as she gigged it round to the front of the building. Here the men from Beacon Ridge sat their mounts, Jake Enderby holding the deputy U.S. marshal's big chestnut gelding and the wiry-looking grey cow pony which was almost certainly Fred Buck's horse.

'Let Wells have the spare,' Aldridge ordered, removing his own horse from Jake Enderby's care.

Wells took the cow pony's reins from Jake's hand. He noted the empty rifle holster on the brute's saddle, and remembered that Buck had lost his gun at the time of being wounded. He thrust his own Winchester into the scabbard, then stepped astride the horse. Watching the men from Beacon Ridge form up around Joan Hastings, he let the party turn, then rode to the front, where Aldridge had taken up the lead position, and placed his mount beside the lawman's.

Aldridge said: 'You know the way, Wells, and seem to have got everything cut-and-dried. Lead us, please, to the Broken S ranch house.'

'Yes, sir,' Wells said, and pointed in an easterly direction as he heeled at the grey.

They left the shack's foreground at a good clip. Wells avoided the landfolds of the northern plain, and kept to the right and the flattest going in the vicinity. He led the party round the southern side of the hillock from which he had first spotted the line shack and then straight down the country. Before them was a fine view of the crags that bordered the twenty mile distant Prairie river, though Wells hardly considered it and doubted that his companions did either. This was no joyride; there could still be tragedy at the end of it. The criminals involved were in too deep to give up easily. Everybody seemed to realize that, and it made the party's mood increasingly grim.

The miles fell behind them, and they neared the heart of the ranch. Here the Spearman herds were thick upon the ground. Cows got in their path occasionally and the odd bull threatened to charge them, but of men they saw nothing, and Wells was beginning to wonder whether the Broken S had actually lost the capacity to form a reception committee, when the well-broken ring of buildings on the Spearman ranch site became visible low upon the land a mile or two ahead.

'That where we're going?' Aldridge asked.

'That's it,' Wells responded.

'We seem to be getting away with it nicely,' the lawman reflected. 'I expect Amos Spearman has been told that it's the Federal Law he's dealing with now.'

'Maybe,' Wells said doubtfully. 'We're not out of the wood yet. Nor should you put too much of the blame on the general. From what I've seen, his missus is allowed the biggest say.'

'My office might say you were trying to excuse an old friend,' Aldridge said insidiously.

'A friend he is, Marshal,' Wells said emphatically. 'But I wouldn't try to excuse him on that account. I accept my friends as they are. Spearman can be an ornery old goat — especially when he believes he's in the right, as he does here. He's not innocent. He's given the nod to bullying and arson. But it's my belief the real bad doings have been engineered behind the scenes

221

by that wife of his.'

'How about a signed statement to that effect?' the lawman asked.

'It's an opinion,' Wells admitted. 'Offered in mitigation.'

'All very well in court,' Aldridge commented. 'But not likely to keep the man out of it.'

'I reckon I've said as much as I can say,' Wells said resignedly, his eye picking up a tiny flash of metal at the front edge of a natural entrenchment in the range about two hundred yards ahead. 'Whoa up, Marshal!'

'What's the matter?' Aldridge asked tautly, reining in.

'There's a kind of trench up front,' Wells replied. 'If I didn't spot a gun barrel peeping out of there just now, I'll eat my hat. I reckon that's where the reception committee is lying in wait.'

'All right,' the lawman acknowledged, cupping his hands to his mouth. 'We know you're there, boys! Put up your guns, and show yourselves!'

Heads lifted out of the trench. Wells

concentrated on the faces now in sight, and was soon sure that neither Jack Straw's nor any others belonging to the Broken S's surviving hired gunmen were present. The men blocking the path to the ranch yard were ordinary cowboys and unlikely to risk opening fire once they knew the Federal Law had arrived. 'Tell them who you are, Marshal,' Wells advised.

'I'm Deputy U.S. Marshal Cuthbert Aldridge,' the lawman announced, 'out of the Fort Worth office. I have business with Amos Spearman, owner of the Broken S ranch. If you obstruct me, you obstruct the United States Judiciary, and that's an offence punishable by a jail sentence. If you want to avoid trouble, all you have to do is behave peaceably and let me and my posse through. It's up to you.'

'Deputy U.S. marshal, did you say?' demanded a harsh voice from the trench.

'That's what I said,' Aldridge responded. 'Don't try it on. You heard me well enough! What's *your* name?'

'Mind your own business!' the harsh voice answered. 'Take yourself off, Aldridge! There must be some place you're welcome!'

'I've stated my business,' the lawman retorted, 'and I mean to see it through. Either come up out of that trench and stand aside, or start shooting. But remember what I told you. If you start shooting, it's prison for one and all!'

'You're as dumb as most o' your kind!' came the rejoinder. 'Supposin' we kill the lot of you? How about that?'

'I'll become an army,' Aldridge warned. 'The days are over when cattlemen could make their own laws and generally ride roughshod. You boys might as well accept it, and get on with your work.' He paused, obviously calculating. 'Don't listen to that loudmouth who thinks he's speaking for you. I'm sure you've

all got better sense than that fool.'
Tight-lipped, he spurred into motion.
'We're coming through!'

A rifle banged, though the gunflash
showed that the bullet had been
deliberately fired high. 'No, you're
not!' the loudmouth declared.

Bringing his mount into line with
Aldridge's again, Wells spotted a sudden
burst of violent activity in the trench.
Hands grabbed, fists flew, and legs
kicked in the air. Then, as he neared
the narrow depression, Wells saw a
cowboy scramble out of the place and
stand on its rear edge, holding up a
Winchester for the lawman to see. After
that a dozen or more men climbed up
the back of the trench and joined the
first, signalling that Aldridge and his
party could now proceed unhindered.

'Well done, men!' the deputy U.S.
marshal called, lifting his Stetson.

'Well done yourself, Aldridge!' Wells
approved from the left corner of his
mouth, for the lawman's show of
firmness had undoubtedly worked the

oracle; though it might have been different had the real hard men been present. Certainly three of them — Straw, Colley, and Rearden — were still alive, and there could be trouble from them yet. Others too might be awaiting dark Madeleine's command, and Wells was sure that this business was not going to simply peter out, for some kind of bloody showdown remained a certainty.

Once beyond the trench, the remaining distance to the ranch site was soon covered, and Aldridge's party entered the yard through the gap between the bunkhouse and the stables. They made a right turn towards the house, and Wells gazed around the area which was roughly encircled by the out-buildings. He was disturbed by the fact that he could see nobody about, though he sensed watching eyes and felt minds thinking ominous thoughts. The trouble was there all right, but must break in its own time. He could prompt nothing; only watch and wait.

The party reached the northern wall of the ranch house, and halted before the door there, just as Amos Spearman opened it and stepped out. Halting between mounts and threshold, the ageing man folded his arms, standing tall and lean as he studied Cuthbert Aldridge with worried eyes. 'I feared it might turn out like this,' he said. 'One of my men reported that he had seen a Federal marshal riding in the direction of Beacon Ridge.'

'I'm — ' Aldridge began.

'You're not unknown to me, sir,' Spearman interrupted. 'I saw you once during a visit to Fort Worth. Three rustlers died on the gallows that day. Deputy United States Marshal Cuthbert Aldridge sent them plunging into eternity.'

'I've hanged a number of men in my time,' Aldridge acknowledged. 'I'm glad you know me, General. It saves a lot of chewing over.'

'I imagine you have been sent to enforce Washington's will, sir.'

'I have, sir.'

'Do you believe those politicians have the right to portion out my land among men who've done nothing to earn it?'

'It isn't for me to say yea or nay,' Aldridge replied. 'I've heard the arguments, for and against, till I'm frankly sick of them. If I believed the coming of a few dozen farmers to this fertile part of northwest Texas meant that you would starve, I'd give you my sympathy. But losing a few hundred acres around the edges of this enormous ranch of yours isn't going to hurt you a single bit. You cattlemen don't own the West, sir, and you've no right to behave as if you do. You've kicked the underdog as often as the Federal law means to let you. There will be an investigation into your recent activities, and may be charges afterwards.'

'You're not arresting me?'

'Not at this time.'

'Then if there's nothing else,' Spearman said stiffly, 'the road off my property runs yonder.'

'There is something else,' Aldridge said. 'Is your wife here?'

'You have no business with my wife!' the general protested.

'She's stolen my daughter!' Joan Hastings called angrily from the middle of the halted riders.

'Nonsense!' Spearman blazed back.

'That's the size of it,' Aldridge said implacably. 'Call your wife, sir. If she doesn't show herself out here, with the missing child, inside the next minute, I'm going to use Sam Colt as my search warrant and enter your home. I'll turn the place over until I do find woman and child, because I've no doubt they're here.'

'You're bluffing, Marshal!' Spearman declared, trying to look and sound scornful.

'He isn't, General,' Wells put in. 'I'll be right behind him when he begins that search.'

'Ah, yes — Wells,' Spearman said distastefully. 'I tried to do you a kindness, and this is what I get for it.'

'You're in plenty of trouble, Spearman,' Aldridge snapped, wagging a cautionary finger and all the respect gone from his manner, 'without harbouring a woman — though she be your wife — who's guilty of kidnapping and heaven only knows what else.'

Spearman's eyes were red and terrible to see, but his cheeks had paled and his lips were trembling. 'Madeleine!' he shouted peremptorily over his left shoulder. 'Come out here this instant, Madeleine!'

A figure appeared in the shadows behind the doorway at the general's back. Wells recognised Mrs Spearman at once, and imagined that she had been within earshot all the time. The dark woman was carrying a softly crying Annie Hastings in the crook of her left arm, and at the child's throat she held a poniard. The expression on her face dared anybody to move an inch in her direction.

Even so, Joan Hastings attempted to goad her horse towards the door, a terrible cry rising to her lips, and Wells was forced to twist in his saddle and grab her mount at the bit as it drew level with him. 'Steady, Joan!' he advised. 'It's going to be all right!'

But he didn't believe a word of it.

10

It was all very dramatic, and set the hair on end, but Wells didn't get it. He had no doubt that Madeleine Spearman was slightly mad, but she was sane enough in the strictly medical sense, and he could not see what she had to gain in the long term from this piece of melodrama that she had instituted with her needle-pointed dagger. She had no satisfactory means of escape present, and could hardly hope to retain her freedom by keeping up her threat to the child indefinitely. What she was doing could amount to no more than a defiant gesture, unless —

He sprang down from his horse on the impulse. In the same instant three guns banged from a cart-shed over to the left. Cuthbert Aldridge toppled out of his saddle, as did Charlie Madison,

232

and Les Enderby fell forward onto his mount's neck, clutching a left arm from which blood spilled freely.

Diving under his mount's belly, Wells gave Joan Hasting's horse a whack on the rump that sent it galloping away to the right, with the blonde fighting to control it; and then he drew the Winchester from the saddleholster now at his left shoulder and again crouched under his mount's barrel. He continued this sunken movement until he reached open ground and was well clear of all the animals present; then he knelt and put his rifle to his shoulder, drawing the hammer on a cartridge that he knew to be already in its barrel.

His sights met on a face that had revealed too much of itself above the front wall of a waggon which stood as the middle of three that were positioned across the open face of the shed from which the shots had just issued. He was fairly sure that his target was Sam Colley, and squeezed the trigger more in expectation of scaring the man than killing him, but he evidently sent his bullet into Colley's brain, for the hardcase's jaw fell forward onto the timber behind the driving board and his eyes went on staring vacantly out into the ranch yard.

Preparing for a second shot, Wells saw a man's head and shoulders rise into view beside the slumped Colley. This second individual began a swift examination of his shot comrade and, clearly shocked to find that Colley was dead, looked straight towards Wells and the rifle that had done the killing. Wells triggered again, and his slug sent the man opposite diving back into cover with splinters off the top of the waggon leaping about him.

There was a brief pause. The frightened man's face appeared again, then vanished. Wells frowned over the fellow's identity. The other was neither Rearden nor Straw; he'd swear to that. In fact, now he came to think of it, the man had the looks of Al Sharp, another of the men originally hired for their guns. Flicking the ejector again, Wells considered the matter carefully; for there could be something of vital importance here. To begin with, three rifles had fired from the cart-shed. He had eliminated Colley, and scared Sharp, but so far been given no glimpse of the third rifleman. The chances were the fellow was either Straw or Rearden; but he must be sure which one; and then he was sure, for it was Rearden's large and ugly head behind the Winchester that suddenly thrust into view and set the dirt kicking about him.

Wells let Rearden have a bullet in reply, asking himself, as the big man across the way ducked abruptly, what had become of Jack Straw. Was the assassin still around? Or had he, according to his habit, slipped quietly away when he saw his safety ebbing? But Wells could not believe that Madeleine Spearman would have given him the opportunity to slide off that easily and, alerted, he instinctively looked upwards at the top windows in the wall of the house adjacent, perceiving at once that there was already a rifle pointing at him from up there.

Dropping his Winchester, he drew the revolver from his holster at maximum speed, and rose, thumbing his first shot upwards and fanning the next two; then, as the gun above sounded and shattered glass flew, a torso — that belonging to Jack Straw — fell forward through the window and hung down limply over the sill, hands gently swinging as they released their hold on the weapon they had held and the rifle hurtled down to land with a thud between Amos Spearman and his wife, who still stood in the shelter of the doorway with Annie Hastings in her grasp.

Once more the guns in the cart-shed blazed and, swinging to face the building, Wells emptied his revolver towards the flashing muzzles. Then, holstering the Colt again, he snatched up the rifle from near his feet and drove slug after slug into the waggon where the riflemen lay, closing in with the savage determination to intimidate. And he succeeded far better than he had believed possible; for the hidden pair suddenly sprang out of the vehicle that had sheltered them and erupted from the cart-shed, turning left as they headed for a hitching rail about forty yards away to which several horses were tethered.

Sensing that he had his men cold, Wells ran to his right, following an oblique course and clearing the corner of the ranch house which had begun to obscure the hardcases' line of flight. Then, as the yard opened before him, he came to a stop again and put his Winchester back to his shoulder, aiming between Rearden's shoulder-blades. He triggered, and his shot went true, Rearden flopping forward like a great bear and a cloud of dust lifting briefly around his body. Pumping his magazine, Wells calmly shifted his aim, and Al Sharp, arms reaching, was still ten yards from the tied horses when the bullet sent him sprawling. For a moment he struggled to rise, but the effort was convulsive, and then he, too, flattened into a stillness which looked like that of death.

Wells sensed that he had no time to waste on feelings of triumph. He was conscious that there had been recent movements of an important nature in his vicinity. Turning to his left, he brought into full sight a figure that had previously been at the corner of his eye. He realized that he was looking at Madeleine Spearman, and that the dark woman was still holding little Annie close to her chest as she ran across the yard in the direction of a barn just to the left of the cart-shed. He also saw that Jake Enderby was chasing after the woman, but the man had plainly got a late start and was trailing by thirty yards.

Winding himself up, Wells gave chase too, but he was nowhere in it as the woman reached and disappeared into the barn. His feet slowed, but his imagination burned white hot. The woman had reached the end of it, and he believed he knew what she had in mind. A hoist platform jutted from a doorway under the building's eaves, and beneath it was a fifty foot plunge to the stone loading floor below. 'Jake!' Wells shouted, as old man Enderby approached the entrance to the barn. 'Leave her be!'

Craning, Enderby broke stride, then jerked to a halt and crouched forward, his chest rising and falling as he fought to regain his breath.

Head tipped backwards and eyes upon the hoist platform, Wells trotted towards the barn and he stopped at an angle from which he could still gaze up comfortably into the eaves above. Then, as he had expected, Madeleine Spearman appeared on the stage beneath the bar of the loading hoist and looked down into the yard. There she poised, right at the edge of the drop, and her eyes met Wells' and dared him to speak. 'I know,' he called up to her. 'You're going to jump. That's okay by me. Better than getting hanged. But just set the child down first. Then you can get it over with.'

'No!' the dark woman shouted back defiantly. 'I'm taking her with me!'

'Why?' Wells reasoned as calmly as he could. 'She's just a morsel. Her mother's done you no harm. It's all at your own door, Madeleine.'

'It will hurt the mother, Wells — and you too.'

'It would hurt me if any child were so threatened.'

'So long as the hurt isn't all mine!'

Wells stepped back a yard. His mouth had gone dry, and his heart seemed to be shaking itself loose in his chest. She was coming down all right, and going to make sure that the child died with her. What could any man do in the face of reasoning that was so warped? Madeleine was a true daughter of the devil. She was determined to sacrifice innocence on the altar of her own guilt. She was preparing to confirm her damnation. 'One decent thing!' Wells yelled at her, like a priest trying to snatch a soul from the burning. 'Do one decent thing!'

The laughter that rang at him from above was quite mad, and the woman crouched slightly as she prepared to launch herself into space. But then a shot sounded from somewhere high in the house at his back, and Madeleine Spearman staggered to the rear as if she had been hit a hammer-blow in the chest. Little Annie bounced from her grasp and fell over the edge of the hoist platform into empty air. She came plummeting down, clothes and hair streaming, and Wells could only lunge forward and thrust out his arms as far as they would go. The child landed in his hands and stuck, and for a long moment they stared at each other in slowly dissolving horror. 'Close, Annie,' Wells commented, his voice hardly sounding like his own.

'Hope we never have to do that again.'

The child was too shocked to cry, but her mother was more than vocal enough for them both and, as Wells faced towards her cries, he saw Joan Hastings, dismounted now, racing towards him from the opposite side of the ranch yard. Moments later, with a single glance of gratitude, the mother snatched her child from him and turned away to the left, folding Annie into her embrace and sobbing over her in a storm of relief.

Wells lifted his eyes to the eastern wall of the house. He saw the open bedroom window there from which the saving shot had come. Amos Spearman was standing behind it with a rifle in his grasp. Wells watched as the general put the weapon's muzzle into his mouth, and the next moment Spearman pulled the trigger. There was a loud bang, and the general was tossed backwards and fell from sight.

That did it. Wells felt suddenly drained and despondent. An honoured lifetime, with all its works of war and peace, had just perished in the ultimate dishonour of suicide. Sure, you could talk about pride, greed, vanity; all the deadly sins; and Amos Spearman had doubtless been guilty of most of them. Yet he had also stood for what was best in the human race. How could you average the thing out? Except to say that it was all in a lifetime. But that was a vanity too, for what did any lifetime matter? The wind would howl through the ruins of the era, and the dust would blow; and a century from now a later race of men would look at the remains of what Spearman had built, wonder a moment — and then shrug.

Just then Wells saw Jake Enderby come out of the barn. He had not even been aware that the other had entered the building. Then, realizing why Enderby had gone in, Wells raised a questioning eyebrow.

'She's dead,' Jake said.

Wells nodded. He hadn't imagined

it would be otherwise. The general had been an excellent shot, and he had been performing both a duty and a kindness when he squeezed the trigger. Pulling himself together, Wells recalled that Aldridge and two other men had been hit in that first volley from the cart-shed. Now he walked back towards the northern side of the ranch house, and was relieved to see the deputy U.S. marshal sitting up on the ground and looking inside his shirt. 'Much?' Wells asked.

'Scraped ribs,' the lawman answered. 'Nothing serious, but painful enough.'

'You should get a spell of sick leave out of it,' Wells commented, glancing to where Charlie Madison was sitting against the wall of the house and nursing a wound high on his left shoulder, while Les Enderby was standing on the man's right and studying his own still profusely bleeding left arm. 'Altogether, y'know, we were lucky.'

'To have a one man army like

you around,' Aldridge agreed. 'Help me up.'

Wells gave the lawman a hand back to his feet.

'I'm going to tell you something now,' Aldridge said. 'You're regarded as indispensable in certain quarters.'

'What damned nonsense!' Wells laughed. 'No man's indispensable, Marshal, and certainly not me.'

'You don't ask what quarters, Wells,' Aldridge observed. 'You're part of the reason I'm here. The U.S. Marshal for the Southwest wants you on his staff. They're shrieking blue murder down El Paso way to get you back. To blazes with Crowbank and that lot, I say! We're putting in first claim and, so far as I'm concerned, you've already embarked on a mighty promising career.'

'But — '

'But me no buts, mister!' Aldridge protested. 'You wouldn't give a wounded colleague an argument, would you? Nor deny him that well-earned leave.'

'I thought there was something in it!' Wells chuckled.

'Why, sure,' Aldridge said brazenly. 'Takes one indispensable man to replace another.' He grinned a little wanly. 'Okay, John?'

Wells felt more like himself again, but a fellow couldn't appear too enthusiastic 'Yours to command, Mr Aldridge.'

'Good. We're going to Amarillo, and you're going to walk all over that putrid local law like a Federal lawman should. Got it?'

'Got it, Marshal. I can do that very well on my own account.'

'I expect so.' Aldridge glanced to his left, then added: 'I see a lady who wants to speak with you.'

Wells turned his head. He saw Joan Hastings standing there. She was smiling now, and no longer tearful. Little Annie was skipping nearby, far more absorbed in the problems of hopscotch than in her own recent brush with death and the tragedies that had worked themselves out around her. He grinned in the direction of the child, then asked: 'Joan?'

'How do I thank you a thousand times?' the woman asked in a low voice.

'By leaving it right there,' he replied. 'The marshal's hurt, ma'am. He and I will be headed for Amarillo, but I don't figure he'll object if we divert a little and take you and your daughter home first.'

'Happy to oblige, ma'am,' Aldridge assured her.

'Marshal,' Joan Hastings said briskly, 'you're bleeding heavily. You can spare the time to let me bind you up.'

'That sounds like a real good idea,' Aldridge admitted. 'We'll go into the house.'

'Permission, Marshal?' Wells asked, suddenly remembering.

'For what?'

'To find a man to drive a buckboard out to that line shack and pick up Fred Buck,' Wells answered. 'I promised to do my best for him.'

Aldridge nodded. 'Don't be too long about it.'

'We'll be waiting,' Joan Hastings said.

Now there was a thought. But it was for the future. Perhaps the distant future. Joan had a dead husband for whom she had yet to grieve, and John Wells had far to travel.

RIDERS OF RIFLE RANGE
Wade Hamilton

Veterinarian Jeff Jones did not like open warfare — but it was there on Scrub Pine grass. When he diagnosed a sick bull on the Endicott ranch as having the contagious blackleg disease, he got involved in the warfare — whether he liked it or not!

BEAR PAW
Nevada Carter

Austin Dailey traded two cows to a pair of Indians for a bay horse, which subsequently disappeared. Tracks led to a secret hideout of fugitive Indians — and cattle thieves. Indians and stockmen co-operated against the rustlers. But it was Pale Woman who acted as interpreter between her people and the rangemen.